Warrior in
by Shannon

IMO BLOCK PRESS

Warrior in Time

© Shannon Curtis 2014

First published 2014 under The Black Gordon, as part of the Timeless Encounters Anthology

Edited by Jennifer Brassel

Cover design by Info Block Press

Published by Info Block Press

www.shannoncurtis.com

Chapter One

Elite Captain Brenda Rowan gazed at the vid-screen in silence as her superior stated the facts of the case, her expression calm as she took in the gruesome details.

"As you can see, Maxwell is escalating," Dresso, Commander of the Elite Guard, said in a low, rough voice. "We need to stop him." Dresso was a middle-aged man, silver dusting the blonde hair at his temples. His skin was still smooth, his body firm from decades of the physical rigours of law enforcement. His brown eyes still shone with determination at the prospect of calling a criminal to task, despite the fact he was older than most of the serving force. You didn't get to his rank, and his age, without being damned good at your job.

Brenda nodded, just once. Maxwell's crimes were becoming more violent, with less lag-time between the discovered remains of his victims. She grimaced slightly at the image of one woman, her clothes soaked in her blood. What the man had done to her internal organs was going to turn her off the evening meal.

"Do you have a last known whereabouts?" Brenda asked quietly. She was already mentally mapping an approach. Maxwell was violent, becoming increasingly impulsive, but he wasn't stupid. He'd have to be approached with caution to avoid a bloodbath.

"That's part of the problem," Desso admitted. "We've kind of lost him."

Brenda arched an eyebrow. "How so?"

Since the War of the Worlds, getting 'lost' was tricky. Universal surveillance, the United Force called it. Plain spying, she called it. But it wasn't up to her to challenge the law, just to uphold it.

"After the last victim, he ran through the market," Desso said, and with a flick of his wrist, pulled up the surveillance footage on the vidscreen.

The footage showed Maxwell, his shoulder-length dark hair streaming behind him, ducking and weaving amongst the stalls at Central Market as United Force soldiers gave pursuit. She frowned as she watched him reach into his coat pocket and pull out a device. She sucked in a breath as she recognised it, her mouth gaping as he pressed a few buttons, fiddled with a dial, and a shimmering vortex opened up, which he promptly jumped through and disappeared. A moment later, the whirling window shrank, the objects around it distorting, before something snapped, and everything fell back into place. The pursuing guards skidded to a stop, and she watched as one of them kicked at a stool in frustration.

"He's a jumper." Her lips tightened. "How on earth did he pass the test and get a transfer?" Not that it mattered, the guy had one, but they'd have to figure out how he fooled the psyche evaluators and close that loophole to prevent others repeating the process. Once you jumped through a portal, tracking was impossible.

"We believe he may have stolen it from one of his victims and jacked it."

She nodded. It was difficult, but not impossible. "How many of us are going after him?"

Desso grimaced. "We have the United Force Summit next week, so our resources are limited due to the security requirements. You're on your own."

Brenda nodded again. As a ranking officer, she was on the coordinating team and knew firsthand the focus on security resources. As an Elite Enforcer, though, she was also one of a few authorised to conduct a time jump solo, and to administer justice across any zone. There were two battalions of Elite Enforcers; one operated in the 'Now', dealing with any threat that came through a portal into UF space, and were affectionately known as 'Homers'. The other battalion operated outside the United Force, tracking down criminals who used 'Transfers' to escape UF law, and were called 'Jumpers'—also the term used for UF citizens who used the portals to escape prosecution. The lack of distinction wasn't lost on Brenda. As a jumper, she was a law unto herself—enforcer, judge and sometimes executioner. With her history, as well as her track record as an enforcer, she was considered one of the best jumpers. Sending her solo would be a more efficient use of resources than to send a duo or small team who could be better utilised on a Head of State security detail.

"When did this happen?"

"Yesterday morning."

Her lips tightened. So Maxwell had a lead of over twenty-four hours now-time. Damn.

She pulled out her own transfer and eyed the vid-screen. "Can you pull up those coordinates again?"

Commander Desso turned to the screen and flicked the vision back to the moment when Maxwell was setting his timer. Her superior zoomed in on the device and Brenda quickly made the necessary adjustments on her own transfer device, copying Maxwell's settings.

"Has he been sentenced?" Now that every corner of the world was under close surveillance, any infraction was caught on camera, and United Force juries operated twenty-four seven in viewing footage and handing out judgements as it was only a matter of time before the culprits were apprehended.

Elite Enforcers, though, were granted special powers in carrying out their duties. They could assess and enforce a solo decision without referral to United Jurisdiction, particularly with time-jumping cases—they still hadn't invented surveillance that could span across the time zones. Elite Enforcers were the guardians through times, upholding United Force law on all its inhabitants, whether they remained in the present, the past, or the future.

"Terminate with extreme prejudice. Preferably before he kills too many more."

Brenda nodded, noticing Desso didn't say 'before he kills anyone else'. Although she could arrive in the same time, Maxwell would already have moved from that point in the time continuum, and he'd already proven what little restraint he had was fast dwindling. She would have to track him down.

She checked her weapons and armour briefly before confirming the settings on the transfer.

A portal opened up in front of her, and she tapped her chest and forehead in a quick but sharp United Force salute to Commander Desso, who responded in kind.

"Be careful," he murmured with almost paternal care as she took a step toward the shimmering space in front of her.

She winked casually. "Always," she said, grinning, and stepped through the portal.

Chapter Two

Brenda landed on her feet, running. You never knew where you were going to land, but she'd learned the difference between a good Enforcer and a dead Enforcer was speed. Wherever you landed, however you landed, keep moving. She'd seen Enforcers get crushed by stampeding buffalo, run over by a bus, and shot by a stray bullet upon arrival in the new zone.

Her boots skittered across cobblestones, and she overbalanced as she heard the rattle of wheels and the panicked whinny of a horse. She looked over her shoulder, then dived out of the way as the wagon rolled past, missing her by inches. The driver sitting on the seat struggled with the reins and yelled obscenities at her, baring a dark cavity for a mouth as he continued down the street.

Brenda scrunched her nose in disgust at the almost overwhelming stench that surrounded her. She sat up in the gutter, then made a horrified noise when she realised the foul mess she sat in, and jackknifed to her feet, shuddering.

Smells, sights and sounds assailed her, and she took a moment to steady her heart rate, to acclimatise.

"'Ere, now, what ye think yer doin'?"

God, where was she? She knew she was somewhere in London, and when she was ... but—where was she? She glanced down the street, watching carriages roll by, the people hurrying past, women in long skirts—and what the hell was that smell? Had she fallen into some giant sewer?

"Ye all right, lovey? Ye'd best watch yer step. Can't go skippin' about like that."

Brenda turned and tried not to recoil. The woman standing before her had lost a great deal of teeth, and not only was her dental hygiene lacking, but from the sour and soiled smell emanating from her, her personal hygiene wasn't too good, either. Her hair hung in oily hanks, and her skin was sallow and spotted, and her lip—ugh, what was that thing on her lip?

"Cor, what's that ye're wearing?" The woman was subjecting Brenda to the same intense scrutiny.

"Where am I?" Brenda asked without preamble.

The woman frowned. "Ooh, ee. Did ye hit yer head, love?" She reached for Brenda's arm, but Brenda neatly avoided the woman's touch.

"Where am I?" she repeated, her gaze darting beyond the woman. A great many people were beginning to notice her, and in her U.F. uniform, it wasn't surprising. The figure-hugging all-terrain suit, made of a tensile fabric these people were still four hundred years off seeing, was nothing like what the other women on the street wore, their long, full skirts, some ripped and faded, most stained, particularly around the hem, their boots looking stiff and uncomfortable. She peered at the architecture, the buildings that were a hodge-podge of timber and masonry, yet still giving the impression of being on an express route to decay.

A rough-looking man wearing a wide-brimmed hat that didn't quite cover his unkempt steel-grey hair started to approach her. He had a red bulbous nose, bleary eyes, and a lecherous grin that spread across his mottled face.

"Where am I?" Brenda turned on the woman, frowning. She needed to get off the street and stop drawing attention to herself. These people didn't know what a toothbrush was, she didn't think they'd cope very well with the concept of time travel.

"Why, ye're in London, gel. 'Ere, why don't you come inside with good ol' Molly, and we'll check ye over ..." 'Molly' darted a look at the man coming their way, and Brenda realised the two knew each other, and the way they were looking at her didn't bode well.

"No, thanks." She started to back away as more people stopped to look at her. Most of the people were filthy, their clothes showing a level of poverty she had rarely witnessed.

Damn. As an enforcer she was supposed to get in, do her job and leave, and draw as little attention as possible to her presence. The portals weren't discovered until 2135, and after the War of the Worlds it was decided to respect the boundaries of time and not broadcast the portals' existence. If you travelled back in time you had to follow the rules. Don't change personal history. Don't change recorded history. Don't interact with a past you. Don't use 'now' knowledge to improve your personal situation. You can travel back in time, you just can't travel back to your time. And like any immigrant, immerse yourself in the time's culture and practices and laws, and generally behave yourself.

She hurried away, keeping her head down to avoid making eye contact with the people who were starting to gather.

"Hey, gel," one man called out, fingering the filthy lapel of his coat. "Stop her!"

Brenda glanced over her shoulder. The disreputable-looking man was hurrying after her, the woman running close at his heels. More men were falling in behind.

Yeah, she knew these people. She recognised the type, had seen them throughout the ages. Those who tried to take advantage of the weak, the vulnerable, to exploit them. She started to jog. She didn't have time for this, she had a serial killer to catch and kill.

She darted down an alley, listening to the yells and cries of the small crowd behind her. She sprinted along, skidding around a bend, the sound of feet pounding along the cobblestones behind her urging her on. She scaled a rickety fence, easily hoisting herself up and over, and landed in muck. She screwed her nose up as she splashed through the rotten food and filth, shoving aside laundry that must have been cleaned because it was hanging on a line, although the state of the garments was a little dubious. She grabbed at trousers, a coat and a shirt as she went, then made her way toward a door that gave under her first well-aimed kick. She hurried in and closed the door behind her quietly, listening to the shouts, the footsteps, as the gang ran past. She steadied her heart rate, eyes peering into the gloom of the building as she tried to figure out just where the hell she was now.

It looked like some sort of warehouse with bales and containers piled in rows, of what she had no idea, although the place had a strong smell to it; coffee, tobacco, and something else she couldn't quite put her finger on, something briny and fishy. She must be somewhere near water.

She pulled out her transfer, listening as the noise of the crowd slowly died away. She'd lost them. She flipped up a cover on the device and ran a scan. Transfers were not only a portal key, they also provided the user with information on the time. She quickly assessed her situation. She was somewhere in London's East End, 1888. Great. Victorian England—but the slum part, not the ballrooms and high society part she'd studied at the Enforcer Academy.

She held up the garments in her hand. A man's clothes. Possibly the better alternative for her to wear in this time. At least she'd still have a range of movement that full skirts and petticoats would hinder.

She dragged the clothes on over her uniform, wrinkling her nose at the smell that came from not only the laundered clothes, but from her uniform. Whatever she'd sat in in that gutter was putrid. Well, the stench would make her blend in even better.

She kept her boots on, but tried to hide them as best as possible. The trousers were rough and baggy, easily covering her terraform suit, and she could still access the blades in her boots, just not as quickly as usual. Her costume was enough to get by, although she'd have to 'borrow' a hat before too many folks noticed the youth walking around had long blonde hair tied in an intricate braid.

She turned to the door once more and cracked it open to peer out. There was nobody around outside. The coast was clear. She stepped out quietly, senses on the alert. She'd made it to the next fence, and was about to climb, when she heard a soft shuffle behind her, and she froze.

"Well, well, gel, aren't ye a wily one?"

She turned slowly to face the voice. It was the man from before, Molly's friend, his face red and sweaty. He smiled at her, licking his lips in a way that had Brenda frowning. *Ugh.*

"Move along, old man," she said to him. Whatever he was thinking, he could un-think it.

His eyebrows rose. "Old man, eh? Not that old that I don't know what to do with a young doxy. Ol' Pete will look after ye, love." His hands fell to his trousers.

Brenda's frown deepened. "I don't need 'looking after'. Go away."

"Aw, come on, love. Anyone can see ye're on yer own. Can't be good for someone the likes o' ye to be alone, not in this neighbourhood. All sorts o' goings on 'round here that ye'd best watch out for. Can't be too careful with all these strangers about."

Brenda's eyes narrowed. "Really? What strangers?" Had the man seen Maxwell?

"Well, now, ye know what happened to that poor woman last night. Wouldn't want that to happen to ye, would ye? Best be coming home with ol' Pete. I'll look after ye."

"I don't need looking after. What happened to the woman?" She shifted her feet, leaning closer. Was this in any way connected to Maxwell?

Ol' Pete frowned, his bleary eyes showing his impatience. "She didn't let ol' Pete look after 'er, is what. Now, come 'ere."

He reached for her arm, grabbing it tightly. Brenda turned her wrist and grabbed his upper arm, striking up with her free arm at his face.

The sickening crunch of breaking bone preceded his cry, and she kicked her leg out, snapping his knee at an unnatural angle. His cry turned into a high-pitched scream as he crashed to the ground, lying in a foul mess of rotten leaves and vegetables, clutching his bloody face.

"Bitch," he wailed.

Brenda grabbed his wrist and yanked up, holding his arm at an awkward, painful angle.

"Tell me about the woman," she muttered.

"Just ye wait, ye bitch. When I get me hands on ye—"

"You'll be in even more pain than you are now," Brenda interrupted quietly. "Now, I really don't have time to waste. What's this about a woman?" She pulled a little on his arm and he let out a howl of pain.

"All right, all right. She was killed last night, in Buck's Row."

Brenda blinked. "Is that nearby?"

Ol' Pete gazed up at her, tears streaming down his face. "Yeah."

"What happened to her?"

"She was cut. I hears it was nasty, real nasty."

"Cut? With a knife?"

"Butchered, more like."

Brenda nodded. It sounded like Maxwell. "How do I get there?"

Ol' Pete glared at her with hatred firming his lips, so she twisted his arm a little more, and suddenly Ol' Pete was very helpful, giving her directions to the scene.

She dropped his arm finally, ignoring his whimpers as she scooped up his hat that had fallen to the floor. "Thanks, ol' Pete. Hope you don't mind, but I'll be needing this."

She turned to the fence and started to climb it.

"Ye bitch. Just ye wait, next time I see you—" he started to growl. Brenda shot him a curious look as she straddled the top of the fence.

"Next time you see me, I suggest you keep walking in the opposite direction," she told him calmly, then winked. "Told you I don't need looking after."

She jumped down from the fence and took off running, disappearing into the night as Ol' Pete screamed for help.

BRENDA HUNKERED IN the dark doorway. Two months. Two damn months she'd been stuck in Victorian London, tracking down her prey. Maxwell was a canny culprit, that was for sure. The man was a shadow, a phantom who was striking fear in the hearts of Londoners. She shook her head. Four women. He'd killed four more women. She'd almost caught him, the last time. Her fists clenched. There had been a number of murders in the Whitechapel district, an area that she was fast becoming quite familiar with, but four were definitely the work of one man, and she'd recognise his modus operandi anywhere. The slit throats, the mutilations. The newspapers of the time had given him a nickname: Jack the Ripper.

She rubbed her hands together. From her calculations, she'd arrived in London on September first. Now, November was slowly creeping past and the weather was getting colder. Her breath gusted in front of her face and she peered through the fog that seemed as much a part of London as the dirt and filth. She was eager to catch her man and get out of this cold, wet, slimy, filthy crime-infested warren.

Maxwell had killed a woman the night before her arrival, and then had taken just over a week to kill his next victim. The two women after that, though, had been a surprise. Two women in one night. She blinked, refusing to cry. She'd been so close, so damn close, to catching him. She'd heard something on one of her night patrols, a soft cry that ended so suddenly. She'd run down the narrow, winding street, eventually coming to a little common, to see a man hunched over a woman.

She'd started to run, but he'd heard, grabbing something from beside the body and bolting away into the night before she could get to him. She was running past the woman when she'd heard the soft gurgle. She was still alive. Brenda halted. Her quarry was escaping, but this woman was still alive. She'd knelt by the woman's side, and only then, when she got up so close, did she see the pool of dark liquid spreading across the muddy ground she lay upon. The woman had focused on her, so wild, so panicked, so damn scared. She'd tried to talk, but couldn't, her throat was cut so badly. Brenda had caught the hand the woman had raised, blinking back tears as the woman slowly died in her arms, whispering soothing words and brushing the lank hair off her forehead, comforting the woman as she slipped into death.

Brenda had learned in the following days that Maxwell had gone on to murder another woman less than an hour later, her mutilations more violent than any of the victims before, as though the killer was enraged over something. He didn't like being interrupted, apparently.

She glanced up the street, then started to walk casually along the footpath, avoiding the steaming piles of horse manure as she went. She'd decided to change her approach. She'd spent the last eight weeks masquerading as a young man, stealing food and drinks wherever she could. She'd fallen in with a group of lads who had taken over an abandoned warehouse. None of them realised she was a woman—or a police officer. Living as a young man in these times allowed for a certain freedom that women didn't seem to share.

She pursed her lips. She missed her own time. She missed being treated like a respected captain of the guard, of having three warm meals each day, of just being herself, damn it. Despite being surrounded by impoverished families, workers and vagrants who all needed a good dose of penicillin and a bath, there was nobody to talk to—really talk to. This was the longest stint she'd had to spend in another time zone, and the solitude, the alienation and lack of just general camaraderie was beginning to get to her. Almost made her consider transferring to a 'homer' unit. Maybe it was just being too long in a place where it sucked to be a woman. From what she'd seen, women were fair game, especially in the slums. Which was probably why Maxwell had selected this time in particular. Prostitution seemed to be doing a roaring trade and with so many doxies around, Maxwell had his pick of vulnerable women.

And tonight, hopefully he'd pick her.

She strolled casually along, kicking the long skirts as she went. Whilst cumbersome to wear, they hid her U.F. uniform easily, along with her weapons. Her blouse, though, didn't hide much. She'd had to unzip her suit almost to her waist, and tried to hide it under the skimpy bodice. She didn't need a petticoat, her holstered weapons gave the skirt volume around the waist—and enough lift so she didn't trip over the damn garment with every step. She'd learned that the hard way. The laced-up bodice she wore displayed enough cleavage to distract even Maxwell's attention for a moment—she hoped. She wasn't so confident on that score. She usually wore the enforcer uniform, and in her time there was no bias between the sexes. There was no need to use feminine wiles, success and career advancement were based purely upon performance.

Now, though, she was giving a different kind of performance.

A shadow detached from an alcove up ahead, and Brenda's heart rate skipped up a notch. The man sauntered toward her, his steps a little unsteady, his outline blurry in the fog. Was he really drunk? Or was it Maxwell, pretending to be drunk?

She kept her movements calm, unhurried, the muscles in her shoulders tensing as he drew close. He passed under a gas light, and she relaxed. It wasn't Maxwell. This man had red hair and bushy eyebrows.

"Hey, my sweetie," he slurred in a thick Irish accent as he approached her. "How much for a quick screw?"

Well, at least her cover—or lack of it—was working. "You can't afford me," she responded huskily, and tried to step around him. "Go home and sleep it off."

"I'll sleep on you," he muttered and grabbed her shoulder. She whirled and kicked him hard between the legs, then ignoring his moan, grasped the hand on her shoulder, twisted it as she spun around and used her momentum to run him into the brick wall behind her.

The man collapsed to the ground, unconscious. Brenda quickly dragged him into a doorway, out of the way of any passing carriages or criminals intent on pickpocketing—or worse. The constabulary were scarce in this area, she'd noticed. She rested his head against the wooden door.

"Sleep it off," she murmured, then stepped back into the street, dusting her hands as she continued to stride along Dorset Street, glancing around to see if anyone had witnessed the 'vulnerable prostitute' taking care of a john. Thankfully, the street was deserted. She idly looked up Miller's Court as she crossed the road.

A curtain moved in a window a ways down the road, before it was quickly yanked back into place. She ignored it. Maxwell attacked in the street. All of his victims had been found lying in the street, and she believed that would be where she'd find him.

She shook her head. London was a big city, and this area was overflowing with migrants and prostitutes. It was a poor area, and something so basic as a candle was used with miserly attention. There were so many brothels, she'd discovered—many where she'd managed to steal a passing meal in the past several weeks. Anyone could be in those buildings back there, the working class of this time gave new meaning to the word crowded.

A door flew open further down Dorset Street and three men fell onto the road, kicking and pummelling each other. More men gathered, flowing out of the public house, and Brenda melted back into the darkness of Miller's Court. She could take care of herself, but she wasn't reckless. A crowd of drunken, violent men wasn't something she wanted nor needed to deal with.

She scurried down the street, ducking into a recess between buildings when the scuffle migrated across the road. She drew back, leaning against the brick as she waited for the group to drift on. A lone lamp in the dark street caught her attention, and she glanced at the building across the road as she waited for the fight up the road to subside. The light shone like a weak, pathetic little beacon in the darkness as it lit a lone room, the golden glow struggling against the gloom.

There was movement in the room, although from this angle she couldn't see much—which she was thankful for. Some prostitutes had rooms in this area, and she really didn't want to see any of *that* activity.

Something dark arced across the curtain, and she froze. A few more drops appeared in the corner, and it took her a moment to realise what it was.

Blood.

Oh, God. No. Another time, another curtain, threatened to consume her consciousness and she shook her head. God, no. Not that.

She raced across the road and fumbled with the door. The handle gave at her touch, and she thrust the door open, her heart racing at the easy entry. It wasn't even locked, damn it. Her heart pounded as she thought about the room above. Please, stop. It couldn't be Maxwell—he preferred killing in the street, but something bad was happening in that room, something that she couldn't just stand by and watch. Not like last time. Memories flooded her, and she ran faster in an effort to escape them.

She barrelled along the hallway, banging and yelling on doors as she did so before climbing the stairs two at a time to the upper level. She tore at the skirt she wore, frustrated by the weighty fabric. She could hear yells below as families awoke at her noise, unhappy at being disturbed in the middle of the night. She raced along the upper hallway, hiking her skirt high so she wouldn't trip, counting doorways until she reached the one she believed belonged to the window she'd seen from below. She thrust her shoulder against the wood, gritting her teeth at the pain, but doing it again, anyway.

The door gave beneath her weight, and she fell into the room. The rusty odour assailed her senses, and she stared at the bed in shock for a moment, before finally lifting her gaze to meet the glazed look of the dark figure standing beside it. Maxwell reached for a little hourglass that rested on the small bedside table, and turned it to its side, halting the drain of sand. He turned to face her, blinking, his face streaked with the blood of his victim. She swallowed.

"Martin Maxwell, I hereby charge you with te—eleven counts of murder," she rasped as Maxwell reached into his pocket. She tugged at the remnants of her skirt, ripping the useless fabric from around her waist. "Charged and found guilty. I hereby sentence you to—"

Maxwell pulled out his transfer and started to fiddle with it. The portal opened up behind him, and Brenda felt a cool breeze enter the room, stirring the curtains at the closed window. She shook her head.

"Oh, no you don't," she muttered.

Maxwell bared his lips in a blood-stained grin, grabbed the hour-glass and stepped through the shimmering window.

Brenda charged, teeth bared, and dived through the portal in pursuit.

Chapter Three

She landed in mud. Wet, slippery mud that sucked at her as she rolled to her feet. Rain streamed down—big, fat, cold droplets that pummelled her head and shoulders as she glared at Maxwell's retreating figure as he ran across a muddy field to the forest beyond. A clanging sound, followed by grunts, echoed behind her, and she turned briefly. There was some sort of fight going on, with approximately forty men raising swords against each other, although how they managed to tell who was on what side was beyond her, they were all caked in mud.

But they were occupied, and they weren't her problem. Maxwell was, and he was getting away. She ignored the hail from some skirted warrior behind her and took off after her fugitive.

He was not going to escape, damn it. They ran across the muddy field, with green, wooded hills surrounding them, and she started to pump her arms, gaining in speed across the open terrain. She could hear thudding footsteps behind her, and quickly glanced over her shoulder. A man was chasing her, his long hair matted, his lips parted in a snarl.

Brenda frowned. Seriously? She had no bone to pick with him. She neatly dodged as he tried to tackle her, shaking her head at the rough grunt he made when he hit the ground. Another man started to chase her. Oh, for crying out loud. Maxwell was running toward the woods that lined the western slope of the field. Once he took cover, he'd be harder to find. Sweat trickled down the side of her neck.

There was a soft grunt from behind and Brenda smelled him before she felt him, his hands dragging at the rough cotton of her bodice.

There was a tear, and she felt a slight jerk back, before the fabric gave. A large hand slid down her back before grabbing at her heels.

Uh-oh.

She crashed to the ground, rolling over as her pursuer tried to grab at her legs. She kicked rapidly, scurrying backwards on her hands through the mud as her foot connected with a chin. She rolled over, rising to her feet, just as the man clambered to his, lifting a square-headed axe. He was a big, heavy brute, outweighing her by at least a hundred and twenty pounds.

"Stop, I have no quarrel with you," she yelled at him, her hands raised, palms facing out as she backed up. She didn't want to fight, but would if she had to. She just wanted to catch her man, damn it. She blinked the rain out of her eyes. The brute ignored her entreaty and swung his weapon down toward her. She stepped toward him, grasping the axe-wielding hand and stepping neatly under his arm. She used his momentum, hitching her hip up into his abdomen, pulling his arm low. The man sailed over her shoulder, roaring in surprise until he hit the ground, splattering even more mud as his skirt flared to expose hairy thighs and the surprising fact that he wore no underwear. Then he wheezed.

She twisted his wrist, felt the bone snap, and removed the axe from his now-limp grasp. His eyes moved, focusing on something behind her. She turned, raising the axe in time to block the downward swing of a sword. The first warrior had finally caught up with her.

She gritted her teeth, rolling the handle of the axe in an underhand angle, and the sword followed its direction. He pulled back, swung again. The sword was long and heavy, and at this distance she was outmatched—but at close range it would be next to useless.

The sword clanged again against the handle of the axe, and she felt the reverberation in her shoulders. Gritting her teeth, she pushed the handle up, forcing the sword to deflect once again. The man showed the whites of his eyes, a wild, uncontrolled battle-rage contorting his features as he used both arms to raise the sword.

She ran at him, ignoring his surprised expression as she bent low, grasped his thigh through the cumbersome plaid fabric and straightened.

It almost didn't work, he was so big.

His weight did shift, though, and his arms flailed out by his side as he tried to keep his balance. She heaved, yelling in triumph as his booted foot flew over her head and he crashed to the ground.

He swung his sword up, but she was faster. She adjusted her grip on the axe and swung it down against his head, the flat of the blade connecting with his temple. His head jerked to the side as he slipped into unconsciousness. She took two steps to the side and used the axe again as a club against the first man now rolling to his feet, nursing his broken wrist. He fell down unconscious next to his mate.

Brenda sagged for a moment, trying to catch her breath. She could have killed the men. Probably should have, but as she'd tried to explain to them—she had no quarrel with them. She looked toward the woods. Maxwell was nowhere in sight.

Damn. She started to jog in the direction she'd last seen him heading, belatedly realising the bodice hung in tatters from her body. She discarded the torn cloth, rain and sweat running between her breasts and beneath her terraform suit, just as she heard the beat of hooves behind her.

She glanced over her shoulder, and almost tripped, her heart pounding in her chest. Oh, hell.

A man rode toward her, long brown hair streaming behind him, his chest bare but for some straps of leather criss-crossing his torso, a sword held high as he thundered after her.

Oh, hell.

He looked like one of the *Four Horsemen of the Apocalypse,* riding through the rain. She started running in earnest, knees high, feet swift, as she raced toward the trees. This one was on horseback, and if at all possible, looked even bigger than the other men she'd already encountered.

He looked more determined, too. She kept casting quick looks over her shoulder, her breath tearing from her chest in ragged pants as she finally broke through the tree line, the horse right behind her, its owner letting loose a battle cry that chilled her veins. She fumbled for her phaser as she darted between the trees, hearing the horse neigh shrilly as its reins were yanked hard to avoid a collision with a tree.

Jumping over fallen logs, she ran, pulling her weapon out of its holster.

A hard body crashed against her side and she dropped under its weight, yelling as the ground rushed to meet her. She twisted, trying to get out from underneath the man intent on using his bodyweight to crush her.

Bringing the grip of her weapon up, she smashed it against his cheek and rolled with her attacker, using her thighs and knees to push him over. She sprang away, scrabbling to her feet as the man rose, and she grabbed her phaser with both hands.

"Stop," she yelled, and his eyes narrowed. He had green eyes, a stark contrast to his dark hair and tanned skin. His features were surprisingly handsome—surprisingly because she was actually noticing, despite the situation. A dark shadow marred one cheek. His full lips tightened as he held his arms out either side of his body. If the gesture was supposed to be reassuring, it wasn't. It just made him look bigger. The large biceps and corded muscle of his torso would be almost breathtaking if it wasn't for the very real physical threat he posed. Amulets banded around his upper arms, and leather cuffs bracketed his wrists.

Where the men she'd encountered before were ruled by rage and the frenzy of battle, this one was calmer, more assessing. He slowly rose to his feet.

"I said stop," she yelled again, trying not to gulp. He was big, maybe six-foot-seven-inches tall, and a chest that would have most of the women of her time drooling. She aimed at a branch behind him and fired off a cautionary shot, the blue stream of light clearly visible in the dark forest as it exploded against the tree limb, and the thick branch fell to the ground, smouldering. She swung the barrel of her weapon to aim it at him again, grateful that the display of fire power had given him pause, and he now looked at her through narrowed eyes.

"Don't come any closer," she told him, her chest rising and falling rapidly as she tried to catch her breath. She started to back away from him. "I don't have any quarrel with you," she muttered. Did everyone in this time want to fight? The sounds of battle could still be heard from the field. Her foot nudged against a fallen branch, and she halted. She didn't want to trip, didn't want to be vulnerable, not to this one. He was large, muscled, and looked more than capable of taking her on. If he tried to charge her, she would have no recourse but to shoot him. She quickly flicked her weapon to stun mode, then wondered if the setting would have any effect on the hulk of a man slowly edging toward her.

His boot shifted, and she shook her head. "Don't make me shoot you," she said to him hoarsely. She hoped he could understand her, but maybe that was the problem. Did these people not understand Standard English? She knew other languages, some human, some *Other*. How could she convince him she wasn't a threat, and to let her go on her way?

"I mean you no harm," she said slowly, loudly, as she carefully stepped over the fallen branch, then shook her head again as he took another step closer. The man was so big, his stride was almost two of hers.

There was a rustle of leaves behind her and breath stirred the back of her neck. Her eyes widened as two strong arms slid around her, and she was hauled against a broad chest, her weapon caught against her body.

She brought her foot down, smashing it on her assailant's instep and she heard a bellow of pain before she brought her elbow back in a sharp jab against the solid stomach behind her. Breath gusted against her neck as the man doubled over, and she snapped her head back. While she made contact with flesh behind her, there was no satisfying crunch of a broken nose. Maybe she got his chin, she wasn't sure.

The arms did loosen though, and she whirled, bringing her weapon up against the side of the man's head, and hearing it thud against his skull. He backed up a little, dazed, trying to shake his blond hair out of his eyes. She whirled back to face the handsome hulk, but his fist found her face first, and she instantly slid into darkness.

DUNCAN GORDON STARED down at the unconscious woman—and woman she definitely was. Her unusual clothes revealed a creamy expanse of barely covered bosom. The garment she wore fitted her like a second skin, clearly showing her narrow waist, the slight flare of hips, the long, shapely legs.

"What is she, some breed of witch?" Gareth, his man-at-arms, wheezed as he rubbed his face, wincing at the shadow of a bruise that was forming on his chin.

"I doona know," Duncan murmured as he surveyed the figure at his feet. "She's a strong lass, I'll grant ye," he admitted. Pretty, too. Despite the blue shadow marring her cheek. He regretted having to hit her, but he'd seen her fight, and didn't want any further harm coming to her. He eyed the strange-looking weapon she'd used to defend herself. He dinna know how she trapped the lightning inside it, but it had near blasted a tree from its roots. Maybe no a witch, but she was no ordinary woman. He reached up and slid his sword into the sheath strapped diagonally across his back, across the small axe he also carried.

"Is she a Forbes wench?"

"Nay, she knocked down two of them afore I caught up with her."
He'd seen her fighting in the field, was astounded that a mere slip o' a
lass could stand up to two fierce warriors as she had. She'd used moves
like he'd never seen, darting in and out, and making the men fly about
as though a wind had picked them up. "Almost like the wee folk my ma
used to tell stories of."

"She's no Gordon," Gareth murmured, tilting his head to the side
to get a better look at her face. "I doona recognise her."

"Yet she aided our cause," Duncan said. "She fought against the
Forbes."

"She also fought against us, Duncan," Gareth reminded him.

Duncan smiled. "That was no' fighting." The wench had stood her
ground against the Laird Gordon, she'd struck him, she'd yelled at him,
but she had not wanted to hurt him, that was clear. No, the little spit-
fire had actually tried to warn him.

"Oh, and what do ye call it, pray tell?" Gareth challenged him as
Duncan leaned over and grasped the woman's wrists. He hauled her
limp body up and over his shoulder, lightly clasping her legs to his chest
as he scooped up her little lightning trapper, handing it carefully to his
second-in-command.

"Why, courtin', of course."

Chapter Four

Brenda stirred. She groaned. Her head hurt. She raised her hand, but felt a tug on it, limiting her movement. She opened her eyes, blinking against the subdued candlelight and the hair falling over her brow. Her wrist was tethered by a leather strap to a post.

She frowned, then sat up quickly as her memory returned. She grabbed at the sheet that slid down her naked body, and clasped the cover to her chest as she gazed about wildly. She lay on a makeshift mattress of a sort, and could hear and feel the crunch as the straw within shifted at her movement. Her hair swung with each movement of her head.

A fire roared in a hearth about four feet away from her, a dark-coloured rug lay just beyond the reach of any embers. She peered at the wooden post she was tied to. It was thick and finely carved, and her eyes widened as she realised it was part of a bed. A very large bed, covered with woollen blankets and a thick fur pelt of some kind. She was in a massive bedchamber, the stone walls stretching high above her head. A tapestry hung on one section and moved gently, as though covering a window. The air in the room was cool, but not too chill, and she could hear the patter of rain outside.

She glanced down at the rough cotton sheet covering her body. Where the hell were her clothes? Her boots? Her weapons?

Something moved in a dark corner of the room and a young woman emerged. Her long dark hair was pulled back in a braid, and her green eyes sparkled with warmth as she set a tray down by the mattress. Brenda guessed her age to be around fifteen years.

"You are awake," the girl said breathlessly, a smile spreading across her face. "I have some food for you." Her tone was hushed and gentle, and Brenda found her lilting brogue enchanting.

She lifted the cloth off the tray to reveal a hunk of bread and some cheese and a small tankard of something that smelled sweet.

"Please, eat, drink," she said, gesturing to the tray.

Brenda eyed it suspiciously. "How do I know it's not drugged?"

The girl gasped. "I'm no Forbes! I wouldna poison you!" Her tone and expression showed enough insult at the notion that Brenda grudgingly started to eat. She had no idea what a Forbes was, nor why the suspicion of such an act would cause you to be called one. She bit into the bread, enjoying the rough texture. She'd existed on stolen food for so long, it was weird, having such a simple fare offered. It was delicious, as was the cheese, a strong flavour that rolled over the palate in a vigorous wave.

"What is your name?" Brenda asked. Perhaps this young woman could release her, and she could somehow continue her pursuit of Maxwell. She hated to think of the lead her fugitive might have already.

"I am Myrtle, of the clan Gordon," she said shyly, smiling. "And you?"

"I am Brenda Rowan," she responded and couldn't resist smiling in return.

Myrtle frowned as she thought for a moment. "I know of no such family name," she admitted. "Perhaps the Rowans are Irish?"

Brenda smiled. "No, I have no family." The casually uttered remark sobered her. She had no family. Nobody to miss her, nobody to worry about her... not since she was a little younger than the girl who crouched in front of her.

Myrtle nodded. "Aye, Duncan suspected as much. He said there was no other explanation for a wee lass to be wandering the hills unaccompanied."

Brenda frowned, then blinked. "Wow. I'm not quite sure where to start with that. Okay, uh—Duncan? Who is Duncan?" What the hell was a wee lass?

Myrtle's face lit up. "Only the most feared warrior in all of Scotland," she answered airily. "They call him the Black Gordon, and folk quiver in fear as he walks the land."

Brenda arched an eyebrow. She detected a warm reverence in Myrtle's tone, just a little shy of hero-worship. She had to assume the 'Black Gordon' was that fierce warrior on horseback, and he thoroughly deserved his title. Maybe not the accolades, but the title was definitely accurate—that dark, long hair flowing around broad shoulders. She frowned, then cleared her throat. "Really?"

Myrtle nodded. "He's the Laird of clan Gordon, charged with the duty of upholding the honour of the Gordon name."

Brenda tried to focus on the words, and not the sing-song quality of the girl's strange speech. "Your name is Gordon," she said, trying to figure if there was a connection.

"Aye, and Duncan is my brother," Myrtle informed her. Her eyes lit up and she leaned forward. "Is it true what they're saying? That you fought against the Forbes?"

Brenda reached for the mug on the tray. "I don't know—what are Forbes?"

Myrtle laughed. "Who, not what. The Forbes are low-lying, snivelling, thieving murderers, and 'tis our duty to rid the earth of them."

Brenda paused for a moment. "I see." Not quite everything, but she was beginning to get the gist of it. "And your ... clan?" She waited for Myrtle's nod. "Your clan Gordon is fighting against the Forbes, who are another clan?"

Myrtle nodded.

Brenda offered some of the bread to the young girl, who declined with a slight shake of her head. "So, Myrtle Gordon, what time is this?"

"Oh, it's past suppertime."

Brenda smiled. "No, I mean...what is the date? What year am I in?"

Myrtle peered at her head. "Och, dear. Duncan dinna really want to hit you, he'll be all sorry he's hit you so hard."

Brenda wrinkled her nose. "I've been hurt worse, and it was really just a tap." If her memory served her well, she'd kind of walked into it. Desso would say it served her right. Myrtle gaped in horror.

"Oh, no, I'm fine, really," Brenda hurried to reassure the young girl. She really was quite sweet, so gentle, so like Emma. Gosh, she hadn't thought of her younger sister in so long. "No, I just ... can't quite remember the day."

"Oh, it will be All Hallows E'en in a sennight," Myrtle supplied.

Brenda frowned, trying to remember from her academy days some of the ancient feasts. "Do you mean Halloween?" she asked.

"Uh, yes, if that is how you call it from where you hail."

"And the year?"

"Why, 'tis 1571, of course." Myrtle placed her hand gently against Brenda's forehead, presumably to test for a temperature. "Methinks you need some rest, lass."

Brenda's jaw dropped. "No, uh, I'm fine," she murmured finally. That had to be a record for her. She'd once landed in New Orleans in 1862, but that had been her earliest time. Now she was visiting the sixteenth century. What did she know of Scotland in the sixteenth century? Zip. Zero. Zilch.

Myrtle rested her hand in her lap, and sighed. "You talk strange."

"So do you."

They both laughed, and Brenda was reminded of a time, so long ago, where she'd sat on the floor with her younger sister, and they'd giggled over make-believe tea. She was surprised by the memory. She hadn't thought of the time 'before' in so long. Brenda took a sip from the mug. The sweet, honey-flavoured wine flooded her senses and her eyes widened. "Oh, this is delicious," she murmured, before taking another sip, thankful for the new distraction from memories best left in the dark.

Myrtle nodded. "Aye. We take pride in our mead."

For good reason. She'd make a fortune if she could bottle the stuff and sell it back home—but that wasn't allowed. She'd have to enjoy as much of it as possible in this time. She leaned back against the bedpost, clutching her sheet to her frame.

"Do you know where my clothes are?"

Myrtle's face fell. "Alas, we had to destroy them." She frowned. "Fancy roaming around in your undergarments. Duncan says you're fortunate he came upon you."

The memory of the dark-haired warrior chasing her down in the forest surfaced in her mind, and she nearly dropped her tankard. Fortunately she didn't spill a drop of the heavenly beverage. She had to admit, brother and sister shared a likeness in colouring, but where his sister had a pretty, delicate countenance, the Black Gordon was all fierce masculinity.

She cleared her throat. "You—destroyed—my clothes?"

Myrtle nodded. "Aye. We needed to make sure you had no other injuries, but the cloth was worrisome." She shrugged. "We had to cut it from you."

Brenda gaped. "We?" she squeaked.

"Duncan and I. Doona worry, we dinna cut you."

Brenda wasn't so much worried about injuries, but by an unfamiliar attack of modesty. There was something about her nude body being on display to that man that made her feel... disconcerted, yes, but also warm and tingly in places she didn't know could feel all warm and tingly.

She frowned. "What about my weapons?" Her transfer? God, she needed her transfer.

Myrtle gathered up the empty tray. "Oh, Duncan locked those away," she said, shaking her head. "He dinna want you to hurt yourself."

"He hit me." She couldn't help pointing out the contradiction. Her transfer, though—she'd have to locate that immediately. She didn't want anyone here to play with it and open a portal by accident. That could have disastrous consequences.

"Aye, but that was so they dinna have to kill you."

Brenda rubbed the bridge of her nose with her untethered hand. "I'm not sure I understand." Their logic was hard to follow.

"Well, we were awful pleased with your attack on the Forbes, but Duncan couldna allow you to attack Gareth. 'Twas for your own good," she added solemnly, then gently touched the bruise on Brenda's jaw. "He was no happy about having to hit a wee lass."

"Well, the wee lass wasn't happy about it, either," Brenda commented dryly. She looked down at the sheet, happy for a change in topic. "Is there something I can wear besides this?"

Myrtle's cheeks flushed. "Aye, we have something for you."

She crossed to a trunk that Brenda hadn't noticed before. The light from the fire only stretched so far into the massive chamber.

Myrtle lifted the lid and drew up long lengths of fabric. One appeared to be some sort of gown, made of thin white cotton, with wide flowing sleeves and a long drape. Brenda lifted the hand with the leather strap, and Myrtle hesitated.

"I'm not going to be able to put anything on whilst bound," Brenda pointed out.

Myrtle sighed, then nodded reluctantly. "Aye, but Duncan won't be happy. He claims you are likely to strike."

Only at big ferocious warriors who want to strike first. Brenda smiled at the young girl who reminded her so much of the sister she'd lost.

"I don't strike lovely lasses," she said quietly. Myrtle smiled, then went to work on the binding. In moments she was free, and stood, relieved to have the opportunity to stretch the kinks out of her muscles.

"Okay, show me what you've got."

It took a little while, but eventually Brenda found herself covered from neck to ankle. Well, almost. She wore a white gown that Myrtle referred to as a chemise, which was overlaid with a tunic that for some reason was called a kirtle. The bodice was snug, and Myrtle bit her lip as she tied up the laces at the front, then stepped back to admire her handiwork. The young girl grimaced as she glanced down at Brenda's bare feet.

"You're a mite taller than some," she commented, then shrugged. "We'll find you some boots, but I dinna have some to fit you at present."

"Don't go to any bother," Brenda said sweetly. She had no intention of hanging around long enough for it to matter. She'd find her transfer, find Maxwell, do her job and get the hell home. Myrtle then put a finger to her lips and crossed to the large wooden door. She cracked it open and peeked out for a moment. Brenda knew a moment of excitement, of anticipation. Myrtle was sneaking around—she was going to help her escape.

The young woman beckoned to her, and they both stepped out into the long corridor outside. "I'll take you to the garderobe," Myrtle whispered, then grasped her hand and led her down the stone hall. Brenda tripped twice and ended up scooping the long skirts in both hands to avoid kissing the stone floor. She wasn't used to wearing long dresses. These garments were different to those she'd worn in London, with a full drape that followed the figure, as opposed to the slightly bouffant skirt line of Victorian England. Brenda glanced about. She didn't know what a garderobe was, but if it was a way out, she'd follow Myrtle to hell itself. Flaming torches were placed sporadically along the length of the corridor, with dark pools of shadows stretching between. Brenda glanced over her shoulder. She could hear some raucous laughter, but it was muted, as though coming from a distance.

"Where is everyone?" she whispered, then wondered why she was whispering. There was only her and Myrtle in the corridor.

Myrtle gestured further down the hall, where there was a well-lit bend. "Down in the great hall," she whispered back. She halted in front of a wooden door that was slightly narrower than the others. "Here," she said, gesturing toward it.

Brenda smiled. "Thank you." She pushed the door open and stepped inside. Her jaw dropped, but she instantly snapped her mouth closed before she could taste the stink in the room. It was a bare room, the size of her tiny laundrette back home. There was a wooden bench seat along one wall, with two holes cut into the top, and the smell... Sprigs of herbs hung from hooks, but those poor cut herbs couldn't quite mask the scent of human refuse. It didn't take an Elite Period Analyst to figure out the purpose for the room. She'd been right. She had followed Myrtle to hell.

She quickly made use of the 'facilities', then stepped back into the hall, cheeks flushed. Wow. So different to the personal hygiene units from her time. Myrtle smiled and led her back to the chamber.

Brenda pursed her lips. It would be so easy to dart away, to escape, but this young woman had shown her kindness, consideration, and trust—and she found herself reluctant to abuse that trust. She couldn't remember the last time she'd just sat and talked with another woman, and not about a case, not about training. She'd liked the experience, more than she'd imagined she could. She tracked behind the younger woman obediently, casting quick glances around as she went.

Myrtle clasped her hands in front of her, a timid expression on her face. "I have to return to the hall for supper," she said quietly. "Duncan would have my hide if I left you unbound."

Brenda frowned. Myrtle was a sweet thing and so gentle. She didn't want to get her into trouble with her brute of a brother. She could take care of that herself, if need be. She held out her wrist. "Fine, just not too tight, please."

Myrtle quickly tied the strap from the bed around her wrist again, and Brenda was impressed by the intricate knot the young girl employed. It would take her quite some time to try and unravel that. And one thing she didn't have much of was time. It wouldn't take Maxwell long to strike again. She idly reached for the earthenware mug as Myrtle gathered up the items, making a show of drinking from it. Myrtle smiled and gave her a little wave.

"I'll see you on the morrow," she called softly as she backed out of the room.

Brenda nodded, although her smile didn't reach her eyes as she listened to the thud of the door closing, followed by the snick as the latch was engaged. She waited several long moments, listening cautiously. Only when she was certain nobody was in the hall outside did she lift the mug and smash it against the stone floor. She picked up one of the broken chunks and eyed the sharp edge for a moment, then proceeded to saw against the leather strap that held her prisoner.

DUNCAN SMILED AS HIS men celebrated their victory, minor though it was. The Forbes clan was now smaller by a full score, and whilst the Gordons had sustained some injuries, there were no deaths.

"A good day's fighting," Gareth commented as he dropped into the seat on Duncan's right. "The Forbes have run back to their stronghold like the cowardly muttons they are."

"Aye, but no' for long," Duncan commented as he took a swig of ale from the tankard he held. "We'll need to send out more patrols. I doona want the village to be attacked, nor our clansmen living in the outer."

A movement on the stairs at the back of the great hall caught his eye, and he smiled. His wee sister Myrtle, bless her, coming back from visiting their 'guest', as she insistently referred to her. He dinna know whether to call the feisty lass a guest or a prisoner, so was settled on treating her as both. Myrtle had been horrified when he'd tied her to his bed. But he'd seen her in action, he dinna want harm to come to his family, and as laird that was his right and his duty. The safety of his family came first. Always.

He couldn't stop thinking about the woman. He'd naught seen the likes of her before, with her interesting fighting moves, the weapons that surprised him both by nature and quantity. She'd been a veritable walking armoury, he'd discovered when they'd unclothed her—not that Myrtle had let him see too much, only the weapons. Some of them he still couldn't fathom. He couldn't deny the blue lightening he'd seen shoot from her spear. Was she a witch? No others had seen her display—he'd checked with Gareth, who'd eyed him as though he'd taken a harsh knock to his head. Which he had—from her. Was she a spy? Mayhap not from the Forbes, but perhaps another clan? He'd heard the Fraser clan had formed an alliance with the Forbes.

He couldna deny it—the woman intrigued him.

Her garments were indecent for sure, hiding nothing of her figure. Why would a woman so scantily clad walk the moors, particularly those prone to battle? The thought saddened him. Perhaps she'd lost her family in a skirmish, and was wandering in shock? Or perhaps she was looking for a protector? And yet she'd fought off the Forbes—and he!

She seemed either brave or foolish—or both, perhaps. No matter—she couldna walk the moors alone any longer. An unaccompanied woman wouldn't last the e'en out there. If she was looking for protection, well, she would have the Black Gordon's protection, now. If she was looking for trouble—aye, he could help her with that, too.

His smile broadened as his sister approached, a fierce look on her face. She had something to say, and wouldn't rest until he'd heard it. He knew that look.

"Good eve, young Myrtle," Gareth called as she strode past him. He tweaked her braid. "Isn't it a wee late in the eve for you to be about?"

His sister whirled on his sergeant. "No' really, but if you be so exhausted, lad, you have my leave to retire."

Duncan hid his smile as his friend choked and sputtered in his ale.

"Lad?" Gareth's expression was a mixture of insult and amusement.

Myrtle turned to face her brother, her hands on her hips. "That poor lass has no family, Duncan. You treat her shamefully."

"Eh, lass—"Gareth said in a warning tone, but Duncan held up his hand. Myrtle could charm the birds out of the trees if she tried, and if anyone could get the mysterious woman from the battlefield to talk, it would be Myrtle. Unfortunately, it appeared his wee sister's fierce sense of injustice had been prodded.

"What did the lass tell you?"

Myrtle's expression changed to one tinged with sadness. "Her name is Brenda Rowan, and she has no kin."

"Rowan? Irish, do you think?" Gareth asked.

Duncan shrugged. The woman had strange ways and strange speech, but he dinna think she was Irish.

"Brenda." He savoured the name, liking the feel of it on his tongue.

"She's alone in this world, Duncan," Myrtle said, her gaze pleading. Duncan sighed. If anything was to pull at his sister's heartstrings, 'twould be an orphan. No matter how feisty and spirited the orphan was. "And I like her."

"She's no lost puppy, Myrtle," Gareth remarked in a tone laced with exasperation.

"She's wandering the moors," his sister argued. "That is lost to me. And she spoke of a hit to the head as a mere tap. I doona want to think what she's been through to think that."

"Let me go talk to the lass," Duncan said, more to forestall any argument between his friend and his sister.

She beamed at him. "You will like her, too, Duncan." She bit her lip. "Only don't scare her off like you do the others."

Duncan frowned. Aye, he had been betrothed in the past, mayhap a time too many. His uncle had organised his first betrothal, and both he and his relative had been surprised to discover his fiancée was mourning the death of a former beau when she'd arrived at Huntly Castle.

Alas, that betrothal had ended suddenly when Colleen had taken a running jump off what was now known as Bride's Peak. He still couldna understand what had driven the woman to it, and if he was honest with himself, it hurt. He wasna such a monster, if she truly dinna want to marry him, he would have released her from the vow her father had made.

His next betrothed, Avril, had hit Myrtle, so that one dinna last long. By that stage, though, his reputation preceded him, and his third betrothal had ended when he'd arrived home from a skirmish with the Forbes, dirty and bloody, and Nancy had fled in fear for her life. He couldna understand it. He had a passing handsome face, or so most of the wenches told him, and he never lacked for company in his bed, but as soon as he tried to find a wife for himself and a woman to be company to Myrtle, they bolted.

He thought of the woman upstairs. "I doona think I frighten her," he said, a smile lifting his lips. Nay, she'd stood her ground and had looked quite prepared to fight him. He liked that, liked that she didn't cower from him.

"I'm sure the Black Gordon is more than a match for a wee, sweet lass," his sister purred, a dimple appearing in her cheek as she smiled.

"That sweet lass has quite a sting," Gareth said, rubbing his bruised chin.

Duncan grinned. "In that, we are well-matched." He rose from his chair, swallowed the contents of his tankard, then nodded. "I'll go talk with the lass."

Myrtle nodded, satisfied, then kissed him goodnight and left the hall.

Gareth eyed him suspiciously, then grinned. "Talk, eh?"

Duncan nodded. "Aye. Talk."

And if talking turned to something more, then he would be amenable to that.

He nodded to his men, content to leave them to their cups and left the hall, taking the stairs with more enthusiasm than was customary.

Mayhap they'd started off on the wrong foot, this wench and he. She'd found herself in the middle of a battle and was forced to defend herself. Myrtle said she had no kin. He'd left her alone in the chamber so that she could awaken without feeling threatened. He strode along the corridor, his kilt swinging with each step. Now, after having some time with Myrtle, mayhap the wench would feel calmer, friendlier even.

He unhooked the latch and stepped inside his room, but it wasn't until he was closing the door that he realised the pallet at the foot of his bed was empty, the leather strap lying in frayed pieces on the rug on the floor.

Chapter Five

Something hard hit the back of his knee, and he fell to the floor, grunting as his knee hit stone. He turned, stunned, and managed to raise his arms in time to prevent the small stool from connecting with his skull. Apparently the wench was no' in a calm nor friendly mood.

"What are you doin', woman?" He could scarce believe he was being attacked—in his own chamber, and by a lass, no less.

She launched herself at his back, and his eyes rounded in surprise when her arm clamped around his neck, her legs braced around his waist. This move blocked his access to the weapons strapped to his back.

"I—doona know—what you are—about, lass," he gritted, trying to draw breath, "but I suggest you—pause."

Damned if she didn't tighten her grip.

He staggered to his feet with her clinging to him like a limpet. He twisted, he turned, but he couldn't shake her off. His vision was beginning to turn grey at the edges. He weaved over to the bed and fell back onto it, her body between him and the mattress, and heard the soft wheeze as the breath left her body. Her grip relaxed, if only for a moment, but it was enough for him to pull down at her arm, releasing the pressure on his throat. He rolled, grunting when she pushed him, and he fell off the bed. She rolled in the opposite direction, arms flailing as she dropped to the floor. She took off running, but tripped over her skirt in two steps. He reached out and grabbed a handful of fabric as she rose again.

She squeaked at his swift yank and fell back on to the bed, and he quickly covered her body with this, grunting as she struggled beneath him. She managed to get a hand free, and it connected with his cheek in a hard jab that smarted. He grabbed her hand and held it above her head, clasping the other hand before it scratched at his eyes, and placed it, too, above her head.

"Hold, lass," he muttered. She was no sweet, calm, friendly lass, 'twas for sure. He'd have to correct Myrtle's view of the woman.

"Let me go," his captive hissed at him, her blue eyes bright with anger.

"Why, so you can attack me again? I think no," he said, sucking in a deep breath. He could feel her beneath him, her breasts heaving against his chest, her hips cradling his groin. Apart from the blurred vision and lack of breath, he couldn't remember the last time he'd enjoyed a romp so.

She struggled against him, and he waited patiently for her to realise there was no escape. She made a rough sound of frustration finally, then glared at him. "Get off me."

"No." He lowered his head. "No' until you tell me who—or what—you are, Brenda."

HE'D SAID HER NAME as though testing the flavour of it on his tongue, drawing it out with a soft burr that reverberated in his chest—and hers. Her nipples peaked beneath the cloth of whatever her garment was called.

Although his grasp was firm, his hold on her wasn't painful. Actually, despite what she'd done to him, he'd taken pains not to hurt her.

He stared at her, his face impassive. In the flickering light from the fire he looked like a dark, golden angel. Dark, winged eyebrows arched over the glittering green eyes that brought a warmth to her body as he surveyed her. The bluish-black shadow of a beard dusted his chin and jaw, highlighting the angular features. He still wore that checked fabric around his waist, although it was bunched between them at present, as were her long skirts. His muscled calves were covered by soft leather boots, she could feel them pressed against her legs. He raised himself, just a little, and his bunched biceps and pecs drew her gaze.

Uh. Wow. The man looked fitter than her commander, Desso—fitter than any of the men she served with, quite frankly, and they spent many hours a day working out to remain battle-ready.

She'd listened as one enforcer reported after a Roman trip, and had thought her descriptions fanciful and exaggerated of the men of that time, but now Brenda wondered if the enforcer's stories were entirely fiction, or if, in fact, there was some truth to them.

This man was gorgeous. That chest, those scored abs...she swallowed. Yeah, he was hot. His gaze slid from her eyes and halted at her mouth for a moment, before slowly touring over her, pausing briefly at her breasts.

Her nipples pebbled at his scrutiny, and the sensual light in his green eyes flared before following the line of her body to the point where his groin pressed against hers. The man unsettled her. She wasn't used to being scrutinised by men. She was an officer, a highly-ranked, lethally-trained officer accustomed to being treated with the respect due her station. Sure, she'd had some partners when going through the academy, but the life of an enforcer was a lonely one. The constant travelling, the long absences, the high mortality rate. She couldn't remember the last time she'd lain in a man's arms.

Damn it, she wasn't 'lying in his arms'. He was holding her captive, he was keeping her from completing her mission, he was—quite possibly the sexiest man of all times.

She eyed his arms. Strong arms, sexy arms. His hands were massive, too. She quietly wondered if all of him was massive, then frowned. What was wrong with her? Was there something about the atmosphere of this time? Some element in the air she breathed that had her fantasising about a well-muscled hunk—what he might, or might not be wearing under his skirt—turning her into a puddle of wanton mush? The way he looked at her, all slumberous and heavy-lidded, suggested he, too, felt some of the bizarre physical desire arcing between them, yet he seemed perfectly fine with it. Actually, he looked like he was enjoying it, revelling in it.

She tried to calm herself, difficult to do when she just wanted to relax into his hold, widen her legs and do some field research. Her eyes widened. Er, was that him? Despite the folds of her outfit, and the cloth of his, she could feel a distinct bulge growing between them. She swallowed. He felt—huge.

"I need to go," she told him quietly. Every second she spent lusting after the warrior between her legs was extra time for Maxwell to get away.

"I'd like you to stay."

His voice was a low, deep rumble, and some dormant part of her body slowly awakened. A part that really should go back to sleep until after she found Maxwell.

"You can't keep me here," she said, trying to inject strength into her protest. "You have no right."

"Ah, but a woman travelling alone needs protection."

She frowned. "You think kidnapping me and holding me prisoner is protection?" Did he hear the contradiction in his words?

He nodded. "Aye. The battlefield is no place for a wee woman. I had to stop you afore you hurt yourself or got yourself killed."

Her mouth opened. A wee woman? "I'm not so wee," she bristled. She was five-foot-nine inches, taller than some of her male colleagues. "And I can take care of myself." He talked as though women were inferior, damn it. "Current position notwithstanding," she muttered. "Can you please get off me? This makes me uncomfortable." And hot. Horny, too.

His lips quirked. His lips were full and decidedly sexy, looking pink and soft and kissable, his strong jaw dusted with dark hair. "Will you strike at me again?"

Probably. The man was gorgeous, but also condescending and infuriating. "No," she said. It wasn't a complete lie. She needed some information first, but she would do whatever it took to gain her freedom and complete her mission. Her gaze dropped to his lips. They looked so supple and warm, and she was so tempted to press her mouth against his, to feel just how supple and warm they were. He eyed her for a moment, as though he knew exactly what was going on in her mind and how easily he could distract her, if need be. As though he knew exactly how kissable his lips looked, how melt-in-his-arms hot he was, damn it. After a moment he levered himself off of her, and her eyes widened as his hardness brushed momentarily against her core with his movement, flooding her with a liquid warmth. He rose from the bed, but didn't wander far, as though not trusting her enough to give her too much space.

She almost wanted him to pounce on her again. Maybe there was something in the water. Mead. Whatever.

"Where are my weapons?" she asked, sitting up in the bed. She'd feel a lot more comfortable having this conversation if she was armed.

The handsome hulk leaned against the upright post of the bed. "Aye, 'tis a good question, that. How came you to have these weapons on your person? 'Tis a miracle you dinna harm yourself," he said, shaking his head as his dark brows pulled together.

"Where are they?" she asked again, choosing to ignore his condescension. Didn't women defend themselves in this time? His eyes were bright with curiosity. From what she'd seen on that battlefield, her weapons would raise questions. She had to weigh up how much information she could divulge. She'd had to rescue some enforcers from institutions for the insane, when they'd shared the truth of their origins and been presumed mad. She didn't want to wind up in a crazy house, or worse, executed. By her reckoning, electricity was still another three hundred years away, so time travel would be a difficult concept to sell.

He folded his arms. "I'm afraid they were destroyed," he responded. Funny, he didn't look in the least apologetic.

"Destroyed?" she said weakly. She couldn't remember the last time she was without her phaser, or a blade. Enforcers were always on duty, had to always be prepared. Her stomach flip-flopped. Oh, God. Her transfer.

"Aye." He shrugged. "We dinna know what some of them did, so they were destroyed."

"Destroyed." She firmed her lips. She wasn't going to throw up. He'd destroyed the transfer. That was her only way home. "Are you sure? Those things were all I had in this world," she whispered. God, was she stuck in this time—forever? Training at the academy covered this very possibility, with assimilation techniques drilled into cadets in the case of a malfunctioning transfer. She'd never expected to have to use that training, though. She swallowed.

He shook his head as he slowly approached her, his hips moving with an athletic grace that was tempting to dwell on, if only her situation wasn't so dire. "Who are you, lass? Where are your family? Is that why you were wondering the hills on your own?"

He dropped to one knee, his gaze level with hers, searching her face for information she couldn't give him.

"Worry naught, lass, you are under my protection now." He almost whispered the words as he touched her cheek briefly, and she sucked in a breath at the contact. His caress was light but spread a warmth through her that was near bone melting. His concern was touching ... seductive. She blinked, trying to break the spell he weaved so effortlessly around her.

"I don't need your protection," she responded huskily. She'd always looked after herself, had not relied on any man and although the concept was alien to her, this man's offer of protection generated a warmth, a surrender that was as tempting as it was terrifying.

"Are you a Forbes wench? Are you wanting to leave that clan?"

"Uh, no," she answered slowly, frowning. "Does everything here re-volve around a squabble with this family?" Was that a sign of these times? If what he said was true and her transfer was indeed broken be-yond repair, is this what she had to expect for her future? Constant bickering amongst tribes? Of course, if all the men in this time looked like the one before her, it might be bearable. Might.

His lips firmed, and she found herself distracted yet again by his sexy mouth. "The Forbes are murdering, lying thieves who should nay walk the earth, and 'tis my honour and my duty to wipe them out of existence."

Her eyes widened at his fervent mutter, so similar to his sister's words it seemed to be an oft-repeated mantra. "Uh, I'm definitely not a Forbes."

He gave her a considering look, before inclining his head and ex-tending his arm to the side in what she could only describe as a courtly manner. "I am Duncan, the Black Gordon, Laird of Clan Gordon," he said to her, and smiled.

The flash of white teeth, his handsome features and the devilish twinkle in his eye indicated he knew the effect he had on her, probably on all women, damn it. If she stayed with him any longer, she'd proba-bly beg him to pounce on her—or else she'd pounce on him. She gazed at him for a long moment. The man was a warrior, he spoke of duty and protection as though they were important, that he understood and honoured that responsibility. Perhaps, if she was honest with him, he'd understand her position and let her go. Possibly even help her.... She rose from the bed and held out her hand in the time-honoured way of greeting—the common handshake.

"I am Brenda Rowan, Captain Enforcer, of the Elite United Force," she responded formally. Perhaps, if she explained her mission, he would let her go. Some of it, at least.

He looked at her hand for a moment, surprised, before he finally clasped it. His hand was large, his skin warm against hers.

"Captain Enforcer?" He gazed at her mildly. "What is this?" His thumb stroked the flesh between her thumb and forefinger, a slow glide of skin on skin.

She tried to pull her hand from his, but he held her fast. She frowned. "My rank is Captain in the Elite United Force."

He let go of her hand, confusion darkening his face. "I doona understand. What force do you speak of? Have the Forbes rallied an army?"

"No, no I don't have any connection to these Forbes," she said. "I came here looking for a man."

The look in his eyes changed, darkening with something wicked and appreciative as his gaze dropped from her face to her bodice. "Well, you found him," he said, smiling with a sensual glint in his eye as he reached for her.

"No, I mean a particular man," she said, batting his hand away.

"Aye, I can be particular," he said, reaching for her again, sliding his arm around her waist and tugging her against him.

Oh, mercy, he was tempting. All hard muscle and wicked mischief, a combination she'd never actually encountered before, and wasn't quite sure how to handle.

"No, you don't understand," she tried again to explain, to convince, even though he was dipping his head toward her. "I'm looking for a bad man."

"Och, lass, I can be verra, verra bad," he murmured, before his mouth brushed hers. His lips were warm and mobile against hers, and his hand rose to delve into the hair at the back of her head. Need, hot and fast, swamped her. She sighed against him, and his tongue slid inside her mouth, smooth and sensual and utterly seductive.

Her hands clutched at his arms, feeling the swell of his biceps as his hold on her tightened, pulling her even closer against him. He moaned against her mouth and it was that sound, that sign of mutual surrender to their shared attraction, that caught her and locked her in his web of desire.

"Duncan!"

A loud pounding at the door jerked them apart. He looked down at her, desire and awareness in his eyes, tinged with something more, something vulnerable—confusion? His lips—those sexy, curved lips—tightened at the intrusion.

"Duncan!" The deep voice came again and this time Brenda heard the dark note of urgency.

"Aye, Gareth?" Duncan's arms dropped from her and he stepped away toward the door. The great wooden panel creaked as he opened it, and she saw a blond man, another giant, although not quite so big as his laird, looming in the doorway. She recognised his face—the bruise on his chin was unmistakable. He'd also been in the forest. His brown-eyed gaze found hers, and he surveyed her for a moment. Heat bloomed in her cheeks as she straightened her gown with trembling hands. It must be fairly obvious what he'd interrupted.

"What is so important?" Duncan asked quietly.

Gareth's gaze swung from hers to the dark haired man who'd just kissed her so hotly, yet now stood calm and alert. Her heart was pounding in her chest, but Duncan looked as though nothing untoward had happened. She turned away to compose her expression into something more tranquil than the horny nymphomaniac who wanted to scream in frustration at the intrusion.

"You need to come."

"What is it?"

"'Tis Amy Drewar. She's—dead."

Brenda's eyes widened and she whirled around. A woman dead. She didn't know much of the mortality rate of this time, but she had a strong suspicion this woman's death was related to Maxwell.

Duncan frowned, his gaze darkening with anger, with sadness. "How?"

Gareth shook his head, his gaze darting to Brenda, then back to his laird. "You need to see this."

Duncan sighed, then nodded. "Fine. Ready the horses." He turned back to Brenda, but she rushed to the door. He was going to leave her, lock her in again.

"Let me come with you."

Both men stared at her in surprise, and Duncan shook his head. "Nay, this is clan business. You stay here, you will be safe." He started to close the door.

She thrust a fist against the wood, making a small thud that gave both men pause. "No, let me come. I can help you."

Duncan smiled ruefully. "'Tis generous, your offer, but I scarce see how a wee lass such as yourself can help. Stay here and rest."

A rough sound of frustration left her throat and she stepped closer to him. "Stop calling me a wee damn lass as though it's a fault. I can help you." She turned to Gareth. "You've found the body of a woman, not married, and she's been killed violently. Am I right?"

Gareth frowned with suspicion. "Aye, Amy Dewar is a widow and she is dead," he answered slowly, then lifted his gaze to Duncan's.

Brenda's lips firmed as she met the dark warrior's keen green stare. "This is the man I've been hunting," she told him. "I know of him. Please, let me come with you, let me help you."

Duncan's frown deepened and she saw doubt flicker in his eyes.

"Please. This is my duty. I must stop him," she told him fervently, "otherwise more women will die."

He gazed at her for a moment, before nodding reluctantly. "So be it." He led her out into the hall, catching her briefly as she tripped on her long skirts. She nodded her thanks and hurried along beside him.

Chapter Six

Duncan stood in the crofter's hut, staring down at the body of Amy Drewar in dismay. He remembered her from when he was a lad. She was older than he, and she'd been a bonny lass, leading the lads on a merry chase until Angus Dewar had finally won her heart—and her hand. He glanced around the tiny cottage. The room was in disarray. A stool was turned over, and the pot had fallen into the fire, dousing the flames. He'd lit a lantern, and the strange woman held a candle.

He glanced over at Brenda. Her hair was caught back in a loose braid and she bunched the fabric of her gown in one hand as she carefully picked her way amongst the ruined furniture, hunkering down here and there for a closer look. She seemed oblivious to the fact she wore nothing on her feet, so intent was she on the 'scene', as she'd referred to it, holding the candle close to peer at something before moving on.

He gazed over at Gareth, who watched her activity with avid curiosity, shrugging when he caught Duncan's gaze. He had no idea what she was doing, either.

What manner of woman was she? She neither screamed nor cried at the tableau before them, and he'd nearly lost his e'en meal. Amy Dewar had been attacked, her injuries horrific, yet Brenda's only reaction had been sad, accepting. Why would she consider this her duty?

She straightened from her inspection of the door and turned to him, her blue eyes dark with sombre awareness. "She let him in. He must have convinced her somehow to allow him entry." She frowned, holding her arms out as she stepped further into the hut, the candle fluttering in the draught from the door. "They walked in, and then, right here, she must have realised something was wrong."

"How do you ken this, lass?" Duncan asked quietly. Did she have the sight?

"Oh, the door shows no sign of tampering or forced entry," she said, gesturing toward the door behind her. "And you can see some of the tracks in the dirt, here and here," she murmured, frowning at the ground, then looking back at the door. "But why let him in?"

"'Twas storming earlier in the eve. Amy would welcome anyone in to warm by her hearth on a night like this," Duncan told her. 'Twas the way of the Highlands, to welcome those in from the wet and the cold. Dinna she know that? How long had she been a-wandering out in the moors?

Brenda then stepped around the overturned stool, toward the bed.

"He somehow got her to the bed," she said, a puzzled look on her face. "I'm not sure how. That's when she realised and started fighting him in earnest," she told him, gesturing to the torn and ragged blanket. "But he was too strong for her." Her final words were a whisper. "She was dead before he did the worst of it, if that gives you any comfort," she told the men in the cottage.

Comfort? Well, knowing she dinna feel the pain was only a verra, verra small comfort, Duncan thought. He wondered how Brenda could view and talk of such things so calmly—and then try to offer him, the Black Gordon, comfort. He'd expected to have to offer it to her, but the woman was one surprise after another. Brenda blinked, then leaned over, her frown deepening as she spied something in the shadows under the bed. She held the candle closer for a better look.

"Where is the child?" she said, her tone urgent as she straightened, looking about.

Duncan gaped. Nobody had mentioned Amy's daughter. How had she known?

"There is a straw doll under the bed. Where is its owner?" Her gaze swung between Duncan and Gareth, and Duncan could see the panic, the worry in her face.

"Gwennie raised the alarm," he told her quietly.

"Is she—is she okay?" Brenda asked, her eyes wide with a worry that surprised him.

"O-kay?" Duncan repeated the unfamiliar word, frowning. The woman spoke a strange tongue, sometimes.

"Is she all right?" Brenda asked.

Gareth shook his head. "No, she's no' 'all right'. She was crying up a storm when she ran to her neighbours and we've been able to get naught from her since."

"That's how he got in, how he got so close. He used her daughter." Brenda rubbed a hand over her face, and for once Duncan saw a vulnerability there, a crack in her controlled façade. "Where is she now?"

Duncan looked at his second-in-command. He suspected his expression mirrored Gareth's, the surprise, the wary curiosity.

"She's with Ada, a neighbour," Gareth informed them.

"Please, let me talk to her," Brenda pleaded.

"You can try, but she's no' talking. We doona know if she can hear us."

Duncan winced. The poor wee thing. She was all of seven summers and this was a gruesome sight to behold. He remembered finding his father's body on the battlefield when he was ten, but this is different. This was a home, not a battlefield. One wouldna expect to find a slain parent here.

"She's in shock," Brenda said tightly. "I—I can help her," she said, her voice whisper-quiet.

Duncan arched an eyebrow. "How can you do that, lass?" He couldna deny it, Brenda had strange ways, and he dinna want little Gwennie to be put at any risk, not after what had happened to her.

Gwennie was now an orphan, and as Laird, she was now under his care and protection.

Brenda must have read some of his reservation in his expression, as she clasped both hands in front of her, as though praying. The candle fluttered in her clutched hands.

"Please, I know I can help. The man who did this—" she gestured to the body still on the bed, "—he will kill again. He won't stop until I stop him—until we stop him. Please."

Duncan gazed at the dead woman on the bed. "What do you know of this man?" he asked her roughly.

"He kills because he likes to. He selects vulnerable women, those who are alone and easy prey. When he arrives at a new time—place," she corrected herself hurriedly, "he kills immediately, but then it may be another week or so before he strikes again—which is why I need to speak to the daughter, to try and track him down before his next killing."

He dinna want any of this. The killing—of women, no less. He wanted to rage, to roam and hunt until they found the monster responsible... but Brenda seemed to think more deaths were likely. He didn't know what to think. This—he eyed the body on the bed. He'd seen death, but no like this. He didn't know whether he could trust Brenda and her strange ways, but he couldn't not use everything he had to hand to stop this man—even if that meant believing Brenda. Duncan finally nodded, then gestured for her to precede him out of the cottage. She trotted behind Gareth, and he caught her about the waist just before she fell face-first into the mud outside.

"Thanks," she said breathlessly. "I'm not used to wearing long skirts."

Duncan arched his eyebrow but said nothing as they continued to walk to the horses. She'd ridden with him, he hadn't trusted her with a horse of her own, just in case she ran off. Now, she grimaced.

"How far is it to the neighbour's home?" she asked, peering into the darkness. "Perhaps I can walk?"

This time both eyebrows rose. "No' if you wish to arrive before sun up." He mounted his horse and leaned down, offering his hand. She eyed the horse for a moment, then swallowed.

"Doona tell me you're afraid of a horse?" he exclaimed. She'd just been inside a hut with a corpse and she baulked at getting on the horse? Or was sharing the saddle with him the problem? He'd been a perfect gentleman on the ride out, focused on the problem of a dead woman who shouldna be dead at all, despite the distraction the sweet temptation her body provided.

She lifted her chin. "I'm not afraid," she said, her eyes darting to the horse's head. He hid his smile. She was a poor liar.

"Come on, lass."

She reluctantly placed her hand in his and let him pull her up in front of him. He caught her as she leaned back and nearly fell over the other side of the horse. Gareth coughed behind him.

"What are you doing, lass?" He couldn't hide the surprise in his voice as she weaved dangerously to the side again, and he had to grasp her tight.

"I'm trying to get my leg over." She again tried to lift her leg, batting at the folds in her skirt, and displaying an immodest amount of leg. He stopped her, ignoring the wheezing coming from his man-at-arms.

"Why, lass?"

"So I can sit like you," she told him, her tone suggesting the reason behind her actions were obvious.

"You can sit just as you are," he said, scooping her closer to his lap and urging his horse into a walk.

She squealed, ever so briefly, then clutched at his arms.

"Anyone would think you've never ridden a horse before," he muttered.

"Anyone would be right," she muttered back.

The horse began to trot, and her grip on him tightened. He smiled and nudged the horse into a canter, enjoying the contact as she tried to glue her body to his.

BRENDA SAGGED AGAINST the wooden door, exhausted. Duncan eyed her grimly for a moment, before gesturing to the pallet on the floor at the end of his bed. "Rest, lass. You've done all you can for tonight." He slid his arm behind her, and she quickly moved out of his way as he locked the door. "Just in case," he whispered, winking.

In case of what? In case she managed to escape him and continue with her search of Maxwell? Or in case she couldn't keep her hands to herself and tried to have her way with the 'Black Gordon'? Neither was happening tonight, she told herself sternly. She was no fool, she wouldn't get far in the night, not on foot—and she sure as hell wasn't going to ride a horse. Horses! They were only seen in zoos or in the racing circuits in her time. Here they were used as transport. She shuddered. She still had no idea how folks stayed on the back of one without falling off. Thank God Duncan had held on to her. Her cheeks flushed when she thought of the time on the horse, of her clinging to him, pressing her body into the space between his thighs. She was equal parts distracted with desire and petrified of falling off. And then she'd met Gwennie Dewar, and all thoughts of sexy warriors and terrifying horses had fled her mind at the sight of that frightened, traumatised little girl.

Gwennie was sleeping down the hall—finally. Brenda had managed to get some information out of her. They now knew which direction Maxwell had taken when he left the cottage on foot. Duncan had told her they would start a search in the morning.

"I wish I could sleep in with Gwennie," she said, almost casually. She desperately wanted to look after the small girl, make sure she was safe.

"She'll be fine," Duncan said as he sat down on the bed and started to unlace his boots.

"What if she has a nightmare?" Brenda asked. "I can help her."

"So can Laila," Duncan said, referring to the maid charged with looking after the little girl for the night. He pulled off one boot and turned his attention to the other.

"She'll be so frightened," Brenda whispered as she stepped closer, twisting the fabric of her gown in her hands.

Duncan slid his second boot off and surveyed her for a moment. "Why do you care so much about the wee lassie?" His voice was soft, his green eyes assessing. He undid the straps and slid the leather cuffs off his wrists, then started to work on sliding the amulets down his massive, powerful arms.

She looked down at her hands. "I'm not a monster, Duncan. She's an orphan now. What will happen to her?"

Duncan shrugged. "I doona know of any other family nearabouts," he murmured. "She'll stay here."

"We'll need to look after her," Brenda said softly. "We need to make sure she feels safe." It took her a moment to realise she'd said 'we'.

Duncan rose from the bed, his gaze darkly curious. "She is now in my charge. She'll be safe, Brenda." He rolled the r in her name, and she tried not to shiver at the delicious sound.

"She'll be scared. It will take her some time to adjust," she whispered sadly. "And she'll be so angry. She'll need patience." She eyed the expanse of muscled chest before her. The girl would need protection, too, and this warrior looked strong enough to provide it.

Duncan tilted his head to the side as he tucked a loose strand of hair behind her ear. "What happened to your kin, Brenda?" he asked mildly.

"Kin?" What the hell was kin?

"Family," he explained, clearly showing his scepticism at the need for an explanation.

She blinked. Family ... "I have no kin," she answered.

"'Twas no' always like that. What happened to your kin?" His voice was soft, gentle, his gaze tender.

"They died," she said hoarsely.

"Tell me."

She folded her arms in front of her, and turned away to gaze at the fire crackling in the hearth. "One night, when we were asleep, raiders came into our home," she said calmly, despite the turmoil simmering in her gut. They'd opened up a portal and stormed in to her small town, destroying everything in their path. "They killed my parents and my sister." They'd been so vicious, so feral ... in her worst nightmares, she could still hear their screams. "They would have killed me, too, if the enforcers hadn't arrived whilst I was fighting them off. They stopped the raiders."

They'd killed them, Desso passing immediate judgement on them. She rubbed her arms to ward off a chill that had crept into her bones. "The raiders weren't supposed to be there. It wasn't their time." They had come from the future—just like Maxwell in this time.

"Who looked after you?" Duncan asked, coming up close behind her. His hands rested on her shoulders, and she welcomed the warmth, the support. She suddenly felt so weary, so lethargic. It had been a long day, and an even longer night.

"For a while, I was on my own," she murmured. "I'm not quite sure for how long, that time is a bit of a blur," she said, waving her hand in front of her face absently. She'd spent those dark days stealing food and hiding, afraid to close her eyes in case the raiders returned. "Eventually one of the enforcers found me."

Desso had been the one to return, anxious to find out what had happened to 'the one who survived'. "I was then sent to the academy." She was the only child in its entire history to ever be fostered by an institution—but Desso had been convincing and insistent with the United Force administration.

"The academy?" Duncan enquired. "What is this?"

She turned to face him. He'd listened so patiently to her tale. She hadn't told anyone else her story, not even the cadets she'd finally trained with. She'd already told him so much, yet she still didn't think he was ready to hear the rest. "It's where I grew up," she told him vaguely, giving him a small smile. "Where I trained and learned to fight."

Duncan frowned. "I was fostered, too, but I've no' heard of a lass training to fight."

The look on his face suggested he didn't approve. Her smile broadened.

"Where I come from men and women are considered equal," she told him. "We learn, we fight, we live—as equals."

"Doona jest, lass," Duncan scoffed. "'Tis obvious women aren't as strong as men."

She folded her arms. "I don't 'jest'. You saw me out on the battlefield. You know I'm not lying. Give me back my weapons and I'll show you."

Duncan's gaze toured down her figure, and she curled her toes on the rug at the gleam in his eye. "Are you challenging me, lass?" he asked softly.

She lifted her chin. "Anytime. Anywhere." Her words of defiance were ruined by the jaw-cracking yawn that immediately followed, and Duncan's lips lifted in an amused smile.

"Sleep, now, lass, and we'll talk more in the morn." He gestured once more to the mattress at the foot of his bed. She tried to focus on it and not the play of muscles shifting in his shoulders, chest and arm at the movement. So, if he had a perfectly good bed, and he was offering her the mattress, that meant he was going to leave her alone for the night...right? She could only assume what normally happened to an unwed woman in the company of an unwed man of this time. Actually, she could fantasise a lot.

"Sleep—and just sleep, right?" she asked pointedly.

"Were you wanting more?"

He drew the words out slow and silky, and her heart hammered in her chest at his blatantly suggestive tone. He flicked his head back in one of those careless, wickedly inviting moves of his, his teeth flashing in an openly flirtatious smile.

"No, no, sleep is fine," she answered hurriedly, dropping to the mattress. She ignored his throaty chuckle as he turned and stirred the fire, then went to each candle and blew them out, his lips pursing with each puff. She was sure he was being deliberately provocative with those kissy little pouts.

She shifted on the mattress, then stiffened as Duncan knelt on the rug by her side. He gazed down her, then leaned in close. Her breath hitched in her throat, her eyes widening as she focused on those sexy lips. He grasped her hand and raised it slowly above her head, and she waited for those lips to meet hers, even lifted her head slightly in anticipation—until she felt the leather cord snaking around her wrist.

"Hey, wait! What's that for?"

"I wouldna want you to take advantage during the night," he murmured, the breath of his words gusting across her lips. She shivered. Oh, she suddenly wanted to take advantage—and take, and take, and then maybe take some more.

He rose and walked around the side of the bed. She watched him for a moment as he removed the leather straps across his chest, along with the sword and axe on his back, and placed them next to the bed, oblivious of her stare. His hands dropped to the swathe of fabric around his hips, and he started to unwrap the cloth. In a moment the plaid fabric shifted, and she saw his muscular buttocks as he removed the cloth entirely from his body.

Her jaw dropped for a moment as she watched the play of light and shadow from the fire across his golden toned skin. Heat suffused her body, her nipples peaking in her chemise, as she watched him climb into bed.

"Goodnight, Brenda," he rumbled quietly from the bed.

"Goodnight, Duncan." Her eyes closed in mortification. He knew she'd been watching him, the devil.

DUNCAN LAY IN HIS BED for a long while, listening until Brenda's breathing slowed and deepened into a regular pattern. The woman was intriguing, but also beguiling. She'd insisted on Gwennie accompanying them back to the castle—as though she expected him to leave her without care. He frowned. She'd been quite stubborn, actually, and now, after hearing the tale of her childhood, he thought he understood. She'd been caring and gentle with the little girl, and had managed to get her to talk when no others could. It had been hard to reconcile the maiden warrior from the battlefield this afternoon who had threatened to blast his head off, to the kind and compassionate woman who wanted nothing more than to provide safety and security for an orphaned child.

She spoke of duty and responsibility in a manner that matched his own respect on the subject, as though she wore the weight of the world on her shoulders, as he sometimes felt he did. And she was hunting a killer. What kind of woman lived as she did, wandering the moors to stop a marauder?

A brave one, apparently. One who had an uncanny ability to look at an empty room and see things that others could, only dinna notice. Her observations at Amy Dewar's hut were astonishing, yet made complete sense when she explained. She had a way of looking at life that was utterly different to the women of his acquaintance, and most men. Yet in some ways, she was blessedly normal and healthy. Aye, he'd seen the look in her eyes as he disrobed. She desired him as much as he desired her.

He gazed up at the canopy above his bed. Brenda Rowan was an interesting lass, for sure. She was beautiful, she was brave—and she still hid secrets, that he ken. They werena so different. He'd lost his parents when he was young, his father to battle against the Forbes, and his mother to fever after Myrtle was born, but he was still old enough to remember the lessons his father had taught him about the importance of home and hearth. Family was important. 'Twas why Gwennie would forever have a home at the castle. She may have lost her mother, but she now had a laird-protector.

As did Brenda, only she dinna ken yet.

BRENDA HUDDLED UNDER the blanket. She curled her feet up. Her toes were icy, but the rest of her was pleasantly warm. Rough wool itched her nose and she wriggled it. She could smell something gorgeous and sexy—all male and woodsy, and visions of a muscled warrior with long dark hair crept into her mind, along with a languorous warmth through her body.

The muted shouting of men interrupted her fantasy, and she opened her eyes. She found herself gazing at the dark and cold ashes in the hearth. Horses whinnied outside, and she sat up. The plaid, with dark red, blue and green throughout, slipped off her shoulders. Duncan's plaid.

He wasn't there. She knew it instantly, could sense it in the emptiness of the room. She twisted on the mattress, surprised when she registered her freedom of movement. The leather strap around her wrist was no longer tied to the bedpost, its ends trailing down over her hand and onto the mattress as she sat up.

She blinked. The tapestry still covered the window, but she could see the light around the edges. She rose and walked over to it, pulling aside the wall-hanging to peer out.

Men were gathered below and horses were being saddled. It took her a moment before she spotted Duncan, striding along as he talked with Gareth. This morning he wore a white shirt with wide sleeves beneath another plaid cloth. This one was draped over his shoulder and across his chest before being wrapped around his lean hips. The shirt he wore emphasized the deep breadth of his chest, the strength in his shoulders and arms. His dark hair was tied back with a leather cord into a ponytail, and it gleamed in the crisp morning sunlight.

He paused at his horse and rested his hand on the saddle as he listened to something Gareth was saying.

Wait. They were getting ready to mount up. They were going to hunt Maxwell—without her.

Chapter Seven

"No, no, no," she chanted as she raced for the door. She hauled the great door open and raced down the stone corridor, hiking her skirts up as she ran. Down the stairs, through the great hall to the massive doors that led to the yard.

She held up both hands, one trailing the leather strap he'd used to tie her to the bed as she ran toward Duncan, ignoring the other men and horses in the yard. "Wait! Stop!"

Duncan turned at her call, a surprised frown on his face as she jogged up to him

Her foot caught in the skirt and she would have ploughed into him if he hadn't caught her, his hands steadying her. His expression turned amused as he surveyed her tousled hair and wrinkled gown.

"Why, lassie, that is a sweet farewell that will have me hurrying home for your welcome," he said in his deep, rumbling voice. He stood so close, and smelled so nice, so clean. The shirt covered his chest, but she could still remember what he looked like without it. Hell, she'd dreamt about it last night, all smooth skin. His smile turned from light flirtation to something with sensual intent; the light in his eyes flaring with a carnal warmth that swept her from head to toe. This effect the man had on her was phenomenal. She forced herself to concentrate on the fact that he was getting ready for a ride—without her.

"You're going after him, aren't you," she said, half-accusing, ignoring the way his shirt parted in a vee at the front, or how shapely his calves were in their soft leather boots.

He nodded. "Aye."

It was just one word, simply spoken, yet it held a whole world of meaning for her.

"You were going to leave me here? By myself?" Oh, that sounded desperate and clingy, as though she considered him an anchor in this strange new world she found herself in, when she was quite capable of looking after herself, damn it.

"Aye. Where we are going, what we are doing—'tis no place for a—"

"So help me, if you call me a wee lass again I'm going to hit you," she said through clenched teeth, satisfied when his eyebrows rose. "He is my fugitive. This is why I'm here."

He shook his head. "No, Brenda. I'll no' take you with me, no' for this. Stay here, where 'tis safe."

He started to turn away.

"That's it?" she breathed in disbelief. "End of conversation?"

He tightened a strap on the saddle, shooting her a curious look before he tested the girth again. "Aye. The Black Gordon has spoken."

She gaped. He spoke of himself in the third person, as though it was by royal decree, damn it. He had no intention of helping her hunt Maxwell. He had no idea how slippery the bastard was, how cat-like he could be, landing on his feet with another life. If Duncan trapped him, he'd whip out his transfer and jump to another time, and she would lose him forever, stuck in this time until the end of her days.

No. She couldn't allow it. She reached for his arm again, the leather binding dangling over her wrist. "Please, Duncan, let me come with you."

He shook his head as he reached for the reins. "No, lass. Stay."

She was still for a moment, running all available strategies through her mind at lightning speed. As it was, she just acted, didn't think it through. She gripped his arm and wrapped the bindings around his wrist in a single-handed Federale knot she'd learned in her first days at

WARRIOR IN TIME 63

the academy. He looked down and flinched, his expression stunned as she gave the cord one final yank.

"I'm going with you."

It took him a few moments, staring in silence at their bound wrists. His lips moved, but no sound came out, then he frowned, tilting his head to the side. He raised his wrist, and hers moved with it.

"You've bound yourself to me," he said, his voice low.

She nodded. He sounded so stunned. It wasn't like it was an inescapable knot, just tricky.

The men surrounding them quietened. Even the horses settled into a hush. Brenda glanced around curiously, before turning back to Duncan.

"I'm staying with you," she told him firmly.

He glanced over her head to Gareth, but she kept her eyes trained on Duncan. He seemed so surprised. Probably didn't have a 'lassie' asserting herself very often. Brenda shifted, planting her bare feet firmly in the dirt still damp from the rain the day before. She wasn't budging on this. She would not lose Maxwell, not if he had the only working transfer in sixteenth century Scotland.

Duncan's green gaze swept the courtyard before finally resting on her again, and there was something in his stare as he considered her, something thoughtful and assessing, that immediately had her eyes narrowing.

"So, Brenda Rowan, you want to stay with me?" he said loudly, his voicing ringing out for all to hear.

She frowned. "Yes that's what I said."

"And you bind yourself to me willingly, is that right?"

Her frown deepened. "Yes," she responded slowly. What the hell was wrong with the man? And why was he suddenly speaking to her as though she was deaf?

"And you will stay by my side for all of time?"

Interesting choice of words. She believed, though, that her best chance of catching Maxwell lay within the very strong, capable hands of the warrior lord standing before her.

"For all of our time, yes," she said. When she'd dealt with Maxwell she would use his transfer unit to return to her home time.

Duncan's lips lifted in a pleased smile as his hand rose and pulled the leather cord from his hair. He lifted her hand and draped the cord around their joined wrists.

"Then I, Duncan, Laird of Clan Gordon, bind myself to you, Brenda Rowan," he said in a voice that carried to the corners of the courtyard.

Brenda arched an eyebrow as she looked at the cord tangled around their wrists. His was overkill, and not secure by any means, but as long as he agreed to her accompanying him, she wasn't going to quibble.

A cheer rose from the courtyard and Brenda turned a little in surprise. Wow. Apparently the rest of the clan were happy she was to join them. Like, really happy. Myrtle stood by the castle door, clapping and squealing. O-kay. These Scots were a strange lot.

Duncan yanked on the cord, and she spun, squeaking in surprise as he grasped her waist and pulled her toward him, lowering his head and covering her lips with his.

Just like that, heat rushed over her as he slid his tongue inside her mouth. She moaned, her untethered arm sliding up over his shoulder as he savoured her taste. His kiss wasn't tender or timid. It was hot and demanding, flooding her body with sensation. She trembled in his arms at his sensual onslaught, her nipples peaking against her bodice as her core seeped with liquid desire, and she clutched at his strength.

He lifted his head slowly, staring at her with a desire and awareness that took her breath away and had her heart pounding in her chest. He smiled. "Well, then, my lady. You have given me good reason to hurry home."

She frowned. She had no idea what he was talking about. She watched in dismay as he slid the dagger from his boot to cut the cord she'd tied around their wrists. "We have a good direction for your man, and we are on horseback. I'll be home soon."

He gave her another hard kiss, then turned and mounted his horse.

"Wait! I want to go with you," she called to him.

He smiled. "Och, 'tis sweet, but you'll be needed here," he said, nodding toward Myrtle, who was strolling toward them, a beatific smile on her face.

Brenda gaped. No. This was not what she wanted. "You expect me to stay here like a—a good little girl?" she choked. "This man is sneaky and conniving and—" oh, God, she'd have to tell him, "he will jump time, damn it."

Duncan arched a dark eyebrow. "I assure you, lass, he'll no'—" he frowned, "jump time."

Brenda pressed her hands to her forehead. "No, you don't understand," she tried again, jogging alongside the horse as Duncan guided it toward the outer bailey. "You know I'm different, so is he. We come from the same time." She tripped on her skirt and caught his arm, pulling him down toward her, and he halted the horse, waving his men on.

She cupped her hand and whispered furiously into his ear as the rest of his men rode around them and through the gates. She told him everything, all about Maxwell, the time portals, her rank as an officer, and the transfer units.

It took several moments, but eventually he straightened in his saddle and stared down at her, confusion evident, more than a tinge of disbelief, and a great deal of care. He carefully removed her hand from his arm.

"I'll return for you, lass. We will talk more, then. For now, learn more of our home." His tone was soft, gentle, patient—as though he was speaking to someone caught in a delusional world, damn it.

Brenda made a low growl of frustration as he rode out to meet his men beyond the gates and proceeded to ride along the track leading away from the castle.

He'd left her here. Damn it, that man had left her here. She fisted her hands on her hips and gave in to an impulse that she rarely did. She stomped her foot. Mud splattered up her shin and she wrinkled her nose. Great. She found herself stuck in this boggy, muddy, barbaric time without a transfer unit, without a weapon, and without her damn boots.

Myrtle finally reached her and clasped her hand. "'Tis pleased I am to take you on a tour of the castle," she said, smiling. Brenda caught a movement out of the corner of her eye. Gwennie hid behind a cart, watching the whole courtyard with big round eyes. The girl kept glancing around, and Brenda was well aware of her hyper alertness. She needed some care and attention, whilst Myrtle was apparently determined not to let her out of her sight. She glanced down at their entwined hands, the leather cord still dangling from hers, and sighed. Maybe she could escape the castle in the darker hours. If Duncan wasn't going to allow her to accompany him on his search, she would simply have to conduct one of her own.

"Fine—but can I please wear my boots?"

DUNCAN SAT HIGH IN the saddle, looking out over the moors from his high vantage point on Bride's Peak.

"Do you think she knows?" Gareth asked curiously as he rode over to his side.

Duncan didn't lift his gaze from the rolling hills and valleys below, the land he loved so much and fought so hard to hold onto. "I think no."

"She must come from a fair ways if she doona know a handfasting when she sees one," Gareth commented.

"A fair ways indeed," Duncan agreed. He'd been shocked when she'd bound their hands together. After his experience, he'd never quite expected to be handfast to a maid—and it was custom for the man to initiate, but he'd ceased to expect Brenda to behave in the customary fashion. He'd taken full advantage of the opportunity, though. She was an interesting woman. Her care for the orphaned Gwennie had shown him a vulnerability and need to protect that was both attractive in a lady, and mirrored his own family values—whether she realised it or no'.

"She's a bonny lass. You could do worse."

He nodded. "Aye."

She was fierce, determined, with a sweetness that she tried to keep well hidden. He had to admit, he was charmed by her. She also had a fine imagination. She'd told him a high tale indeed, of travelling through time, and being her own version of a laird in time, meting out her own brand of justice and punishment. That was interesting. All the clan knew of his responsibilities, but he doubted whether they fully grasped the responsibility, the heavy weight on his shoulders, particularly when it came to dealing with warring factions and families.

But she seemed to have more than a fair idea of what he faced. But time jumping, or whate'er she called it—'twas a fine tale indeed. Perhaps she was a wee tad touched in the head. He chose to ignore her range of weaponry, the spear that shot blue fire, or that funny little box that Gareth had dropped when it lit up and then promptly stomped on to 'kill' it. Nay, he need not think on that. He thought instead of her fierce protectiveness, her gentleness with those more vulnerable than she, her generosity in her care toward others. Then, of course, there was the woman herself. Long, strong legs, a fine waist and high breasts that tempted him at each turn. Aye, he'd take her to wife. Daft or no', he still thought she was a fine woman.

Little cottages with thatched roofs dotted the landscape. The man they were looking for was somewhere in the area. After what he'd seen of Amy Dewar's body, and of Gwennie's shock, his determination equalled his new bride's when it came to bringing the man to justice.

He raised his arm to gesture toward the range to one side. "I'll start along the western slopes and sweep back over the valley," he told Gareth. "You take another party and go down to the village, and scour back towards the castle."

Gareth nodded. "We'll find this monster and bring him some Highland justice," his man-at-arms growled.

Duncan nodded. "But doona kill him, no' just yet. I want to take him back to the castle so that Brenda knows we have him."

Gareth nodded. "Aye, if 'tis your will."

"'Tis. But let us be quick—I have a bride to return home to." Duncan grinned, enjoying the words rolling off his tongue. For at least a year and a day, they were bound, and he was certain he could convince her to strengthen their binding by marrying him when the priest visited next spring. In the meantime, he was going to enjoy being a handfast groom.

BRENDA GLANCED AT THE women gathered in the great hall. They were lined up, watching her expectantly. She stood at the front of the group, her hands on her hips. Myrtle had found both her boots and a thin cord she could tie around her waist, which she used to tie up her infernal skirts and keep them out of her way. She'd already heard the whispers of the 'Lady Brenda's scandal' but had decided to ignore it. Better to be scandalous than a klutz.

"Again," she called out. "One, two, three, four." The women carried out the moves she'd taught them in perfect beat as they fought off an imaginary foe.

"And again," she called out, clapping the beat for their drill. Duncan had left her on her own for four days. Four whole days, damn it. Myrtle had taken her on a tour of the castle and introduced her to the folk inside the walls. They'd even ventured down to the village on the back of a cart. Brenda shuddered. Everything here seemed so remote. A walk to the village could take hours, unless you used a horse—and Brenda could barely tell which end went first, let alone how to saddle and ride one. Fortunately everyone had been so lovely and welcoming in the village. Some had even curtsied. She'd assumed it was some strange custom of the time and had tried to reciprocate. She tripped the first few times, but now that she'd raised her skirts, it wasn't so perilous.

Not being able to give chase to Maxwell was frustrating, so instead she'd tried to make herself useful. The cook had been appalled when she'd tried to help out in the kitchen, and Myrtle couldn't quite understand that not only did Brenda not know how to embroider, she had absolutely no inclination to do so. Stick a needle in some cloth and make a pretty picture—what was the point? Despite their different interests—Myrtle had been aghast when Brenda had wanted to do target practice with some blades against a wooden board instead—they'd shared a lot of time together, and Brenda had grown quite fond of the young woman.

She'd finally been allowed to accompany Myrtle on a trip—again, in the back of a very uncomfortable cart—to the home of a warrior injured during the recent battle with the Forbes, and a conversation had led to her current activity.

Early evening, and she was training the Gordon women to fight. She still couldn't believe these women had no idea how to defend themselves. What if they were invaded? She didn't want what happened to her family to happen to these people.

One maid, Maeve, with an ample bosom and hips to match, put her hand up, a smile twitching her lips. "This feels like a strange dance," the young woman said.

Brenda nodded. "Okay, everyone pick a partner—Myrtle, would you mind?" She beckoned her to the front.

She turned to walk up the line again and Gwennie darted behind her. The young girl had become a shadow, and now wore her skirts in the same manner as Brenda, using a coarse rope she'd found in the yard. Brenda glanced over her shoulder. Gwennie, too, walked with her hands on her hips.

"Grab me from behind," Brenda told Myrtle. "Just hold me, and I'll walk us through the moves."

Myrtle gently raised her arms and touched Brenda briefly on the shoulders. Brenda frowned, glancing behind her. "Harder, stronger," she said to the young girl.

Myrtle bit her lip and her grip tightened ever so slightly. Brenda sighed.

"Pretend I'm a Forbes," she suggested. She'd learned if you wanted a reaction, use that name that was almost a curse.

Myrtle grabbed her, and Brenda's eyebrows rose at the snarl that came from the young girl.

Calling out the strikes, she showed them the moves with another person involved, to an audience of oohs and aaahs. Myrtle found herself looking up stunned from her position flat on her back in the reeds on the floor. It was a basic defence move. Strike, twist, kick, evade. She made them practice the drill, beckoning Gwennie over so that she could also have a turn.

If the girl could feel a little in control, feel a little more empowered, she might start to talk again, perhaps even smile. After giving Brenda a brief description of the man who'd killed her mother and the direction he'd taken, she'd refused to speak. Brenda could relate. She understood the need to crawl deep inside yourself, hunker down and shore up your defences before you felt prepared to face the world. The fact that Gwennie was following her and now participating in the self-defence class showed she was beginning to take in things around her, to look outward instead of inward.

And Brenda was determined to help her.

A sound from the yard had her running toward the great doors. Horses, lots of them. Men shouting.

Duncan was back.

.

Chapter Eight

Duncan dismounted, watching Gareth as he dragged their prisoner in through the gates. They'd caught him. They'd found him near a river, watching a crofter's daughter scoop buckets of water from a rivulet.

The man stumbled and fell, groaning as he hit the hardened mud. One of his eyes was swollen shut, and his jaw was bruised and swollen.

The great doors of the castle opened, candlelight spilling into the courtyard and cutting a swathe into the darkness, and his bride came running out, eager anticipation lighting her eyes. Och, she was a bonny lass to return home to, 'twas for sure.

She started running toward him and he frowned. What in the devil had she done to her gown? The skirts were scooped up, the hem stuffed through a cord around her waist, revealing a scandalous amount of shapely leg—for all of his men to see. She wore boots that encased her calves, made of a strange dark leather that looked far thicker than his own boots—but he wasn't going to dwell on their differences, or the story she'd told him as he'd left a few days earlier. Nay, 'twas better not to dwell on such fancy.

She skidded to a halt in front of him. That was one thing he noticed about her, she didn't simply move, she threw her whole body into motion. Made him wonder if she brought the same exuberance to lovemaking.

He couldn't wait to find out.

"You found him," she said breathlessly, looking past him to the man rolling in the mud.

"Aye." There had been no doubt he would succeed.

She'd reached for the sword at his waist and had half-drawn it before he realised and just managed to clasp her hand before she'd completely drawn it from its scabbard.

"Hold, lass," he said, his grasp gentle as he covered her hand with his.

She looked up at him, her blue eyes dark with frustration and confusion.

"He goes to the stores first, then I must hear him plead his case," he explained.

Her jaw dropped. "Plead his case?" She looked down at the man who had somehow managed to rise to his knees. The man smiled, then winced. She turned back to face Duncan, her confusion clear. "What do you mean, plead his case? He's guilty."

Duncan grimaced. Whilst he believed her, as laird he could scarce kill a man for a crime unless he was certain of his guilt. At the moment they merely had a stranger they'd caught near a watercourse. If Gwennie gave him the nod, then the man's breaths were numbered, but until then, he couldn't kill a man purely because he thought he was the one. He had to be sure.

"'Tis my duty to make sure, Brenda." Surely she, of all people, could understand. She pursed her lips and turned to face the man she believed responsible for crimes he could only credit to a raging animal.

"Hello, darling," Maxwell drawled when he recognised her. He looked her up and down with his one open eye. "Why, don't you make a pretty picture."

Duncan felt his gut roil at the man's attention on his bride. He took a step closer to silence him, but Brenda beat him to it, her booted foot flashing out in a strange sidekick motion that knocked the man into the dirt, unconscious. Something fell out of his pocket, and rolled briefly before coming to a rest against a small clump of dirt. Brenda stared at the small hourglass for a moment, then brought her foot down hard on the small object, and Duncan could hear the glass shatter under her boot.

She turned and started to stomp back toward the entry doors. "By all means, let him plead his case," she yelled over her shoulder.

Duncan stared in amazement between the man lying unconscious in the mud and his furious bride striding through the yard, then realised the reason why he'd galloped through the countryside, had driven his men to the point of exhaustion, and had personally swung from the elated heights of joy to swirling depths of trepidation, was now turning her back on him. Just like Colleen and Nancy.

"Lady Brenda, is that anyway for a bride to welcome her husband home?" he roared at her stiff shoulders.

Brenda whirled, her brows drawn together. "What?" She glanced around. "What bride?"

He strode toward her, and she glanced about her for a moment. The fact he now had a bride had been plaguing his thoughts for the last four days, and his dreams during those nights. She had haunted his mind—and had apparently given him no such consideration. That she hadn't given him the same amount of thought was galling, and perhaps a wee tad humbling. He shouldna be so upset, but she looked like she'd mooned over his absence not one whit.

He watched as her frown deepened, and she glanced around again, before finally meeting his gaze, her eyes widening. She slowly raised a thumb to her chest, her eyebrows rising in shock.

"Me?" she squeaked.

He stopped when he reached her, and surveyed his stunned bride. Her skirts were still caught up in the thin cord around her waist and he gently tugged the fabric down, concealing her legs.

"Aye. You."

She started to shake her head. "Oh, no," she whispered as she started to back away.

His head reared back as though she'd hit him. No? That feeling of hurt, of disappointment and humiliation when they'd found Colleen's body as she'd ended her life to avoid marriage to him, of when Avril's father had told anyone who would listen that the reason for their broken betrothal lay with him and not his fair daughter, and when Nancy had run screeching from the keep, petrified the filthy barbarian might actually touch her smooth skin, swamped him. Not here, not in front of his family, not now—not again.

He bent and hefted her over his shoulder, hearing her shriek cut short as her stomach met his shoulder. He would convince her, damn it. He knew she was attracted to him and he was going to use that attraction to convince her to be his lady.

BRENDA PUMMELLED AT his back as he carried her through the great hall and up the stairs. She managed to twist and reach for his sword, but he was too quick for her, pulling it out of her reach. Her fists were getting hot and sore from pounding on his back. They were entering his chamber when she raised both fists and brought them down hard in what she hoped was the general area of one of his kidneys.

The man grunted.

That's all. It was like throwing pebbles at a mountain, with about as much impact.

He kicked the door shut and threw her on to the bed. She tried to roll over, her damn skirts getting in the way, and he followed her down on the mattress.

"Get off me," she shouted, trying to push him off. It was like trying to budge a mountain.

His lips branded her neck and she trembled. A really hot, sexy mountain.

"Damn it, get off me, I am not your bride."

"Och, but you are, lassie," he rumbled against her ear, and she trembled some more as heat gathered between her thighs and her nipples pebbled in her bodice. Good grief, the man was potent.

She grabbed his dark ponytail and pulled, and reluctantly her warrior raised his head. "When the hell did we get married?" She tried to think of all the ancient customs they'd been taught at the academy. Most of those she could remember involved a priest or celebrant, not so different to her own time.

He raised her hand, entwining her fingers gently with his, and gazed down at her with a wicked glint in his forest-green eyes. "When you handfasted yourself to me, lass."

She frowned, glancing down at their joined hands, trying not to enjoy the warmth of his touch quite so much. Handfasted? She'd tied her wrist to his to stop him from leaving. She remembered his carefully worded, carefully proclaimed response and his own tying of a cord, and her eyes rounded.

"No way! That's handfasted? What the hell is handfasted?" It wasn't something they'd covered in ancient traditions at the academy. Now wasn't the time to discover there was a deficit in her education, damn it.

He leaned closer and trailed his lips from her ear to her neck, and her eyes nearly crossed with pleasure.

"We bind ourselves to each other for a year and a day," he murmured, kissing his way across her collarbone. She shuddered at the hot caress, her breasts swelling in the bodice, begging for his attention.

His hand slid up her side to brush against the underside of her breast, his touch warm though the two layers of clothing she wore.

"I don't understand," she rasped, then swallowed. "A year and a day?" This was some temporary attachment she'd never heard of.

"Aye," he whispered against her skin as his hand drifted to the laces of her bodice. "And we then decide whether to marry in earnest or to part ways." He parted the fabric of her bodice and tugged the neckline of her chemise down to gradually expose the swell of her breasts.

She tried to focus on the conversation. She certainly hadn't meant to get herself married in this time, even if only temporarily. She moaned as he dipped his head and traced his tongue across the swell of her breast.

"Stop," she panted, "I can't think when you do that." His words suggested a permanence, though, a presence in this time for far longer than she'd intended. She would ultimately have to return to her own time and leave this man behind.

If she could transfer.

He chuckled against her skin, sending reverberations to her core, and her nipples tightened to hard little nubs. God, he was wicked, fully aware of the effect he had on her, and prepared to use it to distract her—but with Maxwell's capture, there was an opportunity for her to return home.

"Wait, please," she said breathlessly, trying to focus on something other than the pleasure he was wringing from her body. She grasped his ponytail again.

Maybe it was the almost desperate plea in her tone that made him stop. Maybe it was the hair-pulling. He reluctantly raised his head.

"What, lassie?" he asked gently, patiently.

She was a puddle of wanton nerves, but he seemed completely in control, completely focused on his objective, and this was but a hurdle that had to be jumped before he got what he wanted—and it was clear he wanted her. Which was fine because she so wanted him.

"Where is Maxwell's transfer unit?" her voice was a whisper. She didn't bother to prevaricate, didn't try to dance around the subject—she was about ready to explode, and the sooner she got the answer to this question, the sooner she could move on to...other things.

His eyes clouded, darkening with a wariness that she almost missed. He frowned.

"His what?"

She swallowed. This precious bit of information could get her back home to her own time. "Maxwell's transfer. A small box, lights up, pretty buttons and a dial...?" She'd never had to describe one before.

Duncan's lips pursed, and her gaze dropped to his mouth—his warm, supple mouth.

"If you mean that thing he tried to play with when we found him, Gareth shot it out of his hand with an arrow. I believe 'tis lost down a ravine."

She blinked. Lost. Damaged. Sadness swamped her. She couldn't get home. She was stuck in this time, with no personal hygiene units, where women wore hazardous clothes and the men fought bitterly amongst themselves, where everyone wore skirts and peed through a hole in the wall, and they all rode around on blasted horses. She tipped her head back, trying to blink back the tears, and Duncan shifted off her and to the side.

"Och, lassie. Doona cry," he said, his voice a low rumble. He scooped her close to him, cuddling her against his massive chest as she turned to face the tapestry. "I'm no' so bad."

"You don't understand," she said softly. "That was my only way back home."

He was silent for a moment, then snuggled into her back, his chin on her head. "You have a home here, lass. You're now a Gordon, one of the fiercest clans in all of Scotland, and we'll protect you."

His voice whispered into the darkening chamber, an almost fervent vow, with a promise of belonging she hadn't realised she'd been craving since her family's murders. Desso had been the human face of the institution that raised her, he'd been kind, decent, honourable, and had cared for her as both a foster father and a commander looking after his troops. But the academy had never really been a home, with the changing faces year on year, and the exclusion from the other cadets when they realised who she was—the daughter of the academy.

What Duncan suggested was so alien, yet so tempting, so heart-warming—and so shattering. She would never see the great halls of the academy again, never see Desso again, and would never have another opportunity to repay the gratitude she felt toward the man.

"I know what it's like to lose family, Brenda," Duncan murmured, and she shivered at the roll of the r against her ear. "I lost my mother when Myrtle was but a wee bairn, and my sire died in battle against the Forbes."

Brenda turned in his arms to face him. His tender green gaze held a hint of sorrow, a sadness that was so like her own.

"I value my kin. Everything I do is to keep them safe and to help them flourish. My oath to you is the same. I'll keep you safe, here. I want you to flourish here with us."

His tone was deep with sincerity, and for a moment she thought perhaps everything might be all right.

He lowered his head and pressed his lips against hers, raising his hand to cup her face as he kissed her reverently. Thoroughly. Hotly.

Feeling heart-sore and vulnerable, Brenda opened her arms to the mighty warrior who wanted to keep her in his home. She shuddered as his tongue slid against hers, his hands tracing lazy circles down her back as he rolled closer to her.

For a moment she didn't want to think about Maxwell, or her duty, or what time was now ... she gave herself up to the sensations bombarding her, arching her back against the wall of chest muscle slowly pressing against her, and she both heard and felt his moan in her mouth.

That sound, that signal of mutual passion, was like setting a match to tinder. She wrapped her arms around his neck and tugged him closer, tighter, as their tongues entwined and their legs tangled. Duncan lifted his head to blaze a silken trail of hot desire down her neck to her chest, where again he played with the cloth separating their flesh.

She moaned, rolling her head back as need, tight and all consuming, licked at her core. Her heart was pounding so hard, so fast ... thump, thump, thump.

Duncan froze, and she realised the thumping came from the door.

"Duncan, come quick!" Gareth's voice roared from the other side.

"What is it?" Duncan roared back, and Brenda saw the frustration tightening the muscles of his arms and shoulders, just as it sliced through her.

"The prisoner has escaped."

Chapter Nine

Duncan stood at the gate to the storeroom they'd locked their prisoner into. The guard lay on the floor, the key sticking out of his neck as he gazed sightlessly up at the rock ceiling. Duncan fisted his hands.

Damn Maxwell. He'd killed a good man, with three little ones and a bairn on the way. He turned to Gareth.

"How long?" What kind of lead did the fiend have on them?

Gareth held his torch high. "No' long. Davey was only supposed to do a quick check, and come back for a task. When he dinna return, I came looking for him."

"Then let us search for the scoundrel. Gather the men and let's find this bastard."

"You'll need to gather your women, also," Brenda said calmly. He turned to her. She stood behind him, and damned if she wasna tucking her skirt into her belt again. "The chase excites him. When he gets excited, he needs to kill, and his victims are always women. Gather your women and keep them safe."

She was surveying the room, a small space carved out in the rock below the castle, as were all the store rooms. She glanced briefly at the dead guard, and regret touched her expression. No matter how calm, or how practical she seemed, she wasn't cold to the circumstances.

He made a decision, and beckoned her along the stone corridor toward the end. "I want you to protect the women," he told her.

She frowned. "No, I want to help hunt this prick down."

He shook his head as he unlocked a grate and hauled it open. This was where they stored the most valuable items. It was the furthest space from the hall, and one needed to pass three locked grills to get to this section. He stepped inside and pulled an empty sack off a crate.

She gasped when she saw the contents. "My weapons!" She leaned over and started to pull out the various weapons. "I thought they were destroyed," she said, half-accusing, half-relieved. She grabbed a small handle, and with a flick of her wrist a sharp blade appeared. She slid it behind her back, held in place by the cord around her waist.

He watched in silence as she armed herself, her movements quick and efficient as she slid daggers and odd-looking blades into spaces made by the leather strapping on her boots. He picked up one such blade that she left untouched—probably didn't have enough places in her new dress to carry it. She lifted her chin.

"Keep it."

He turned it over in his hand. It was finely balanced, with a shine he'd ne'er seen on a weapon before.

"Truly?" he asked, surprised. He liked it—very much, but it was a strange gift to receive from a woman—his bride, no less.

"Truly."

He slid it into the back of his belt, just as she'd done with hers. The blade was small and light, an almost inconsequential addition to his arsenal.

"You know what this man is capable of," he said to her quietly, and she hesitated as she tied a cord around her thigh. "You said yourself he'll go after the women. I trust you, Brenda, to keep my kin safe. We'll search for him, but I want you protecting my kinfolk."

He couldna deny it no' longer. She moved with a physical grace and confidence he dinna see often, and only in well-trained soldiers. He watched as she finished tying the sheath to her leg. He may find it hard to believe her words, but he had to acknowledge the purpose in her actions. She may well be this enforcer she spoke of.

She nodded. "Fine," she said abruptly. "I'll do it."

He could tell the restraint chafed at her, but he could also see she realised and accepted the responsibility and trust he'd placed in her. She slid a wicked-looking blade into the sheath and was reaching for the spear that spat blue flame. He reached over and halted her movement.

"No' that one," he told her quietly. It was too foreign, too hard to explain, and he dinna understand its workings, wasna sure how safe it was to be used around his kinfolk. She met his gaze, and he saw she was trying to read his expression. A faint line appeared on her brow, then understanding flared in the depths of her blue gaze.

She nodded. "Let's roll," she said, and preceded him out of the storeroom.

He arched an eyebrow as he followed her. Roll? He dinna understand—she was walking on her two feet, and apart from the mesmerising swing of her hips in the hiked up skirt, there was no rolling to be done. Unless she meant rolling as they had in his bed upstairs?

He slid his arm around her waist and pulled her to him, turning her to face him as he did so. He lowered his head and kissed her, taking full advantage of her surprised gasp to gain access to her mouth. He kissed her thoroughly, quickly, enjoying the texture and flavour of her mouth.

"Take care," he whispered against her lips, and he felt her smile.

"Always."

BRENDA HERDED THE WOMEN into one of the larger chambers. Apparently the room, and its attached solar, had once belonged to Duncan's mother. She nodded at each of the women, reading their confused and fearful expressions on their faces. She didn't think they'd experienced a lockdown before, and from Gareth's suggestion, apart from the storerooms below the castle, this was the next best place to hide a gaggle of women, as he put it.

"We'll be fine," she reassured them. She felt a little hand tug at her skirt and she glanced down, smiling in relief when she saw Gwennie, until she noticed the terror on the little girl's face. She quickly knelt down to hug the child.

"Hey, we're fine, sweetie. We're safe, and we're just going to sit here and chat and play some games with all the other little ones here," she said. She noticed Deirdre, Davy's pregnant wife. She was sobbing quietly in a corner, clutching three little children close to her swollen belly as others tried to comfort her. She'd been informed of her husband's murder.

Gwennie's hold tightened and Brenda could feel the child trembling in her arms. She pulled back so she could meet the girl's gaze. "I won't let anything happen to you," she promised calmly. Maxwell would have to kill her to get anywhere near these women, the same women who had laughed and joked with her over the last few days, had shown her all manner of things from how to dress to how to tend to a wounded warrior, and to whom she had shown defence moves.

"Okay, everybody. We are safe here, but we can make ourselves safer. Are there any other access points to this area?"

Maeve looked at her in confusion. "Access points?"

"Ways in," Brenda explained hurriedly.

"Nay."

She started to walk around the solar. The room was round and well-placed in the tower. She glanced out what passed for windows in this time, the long and narrow slits in the wall. She could clearly see the yard below, the stables and the bailey. Some of the men had gathered in the yard, and now split up and took several different directions.

She turned to face the women. "Okay, let's get organised. First, look for anything you can use as a weapon."

The women hurried around the room, opening drawers and doors, and pulling out whatever they could put their hands on. Brenda nodded in approval at what they found—needles, scissors, some small blades, a wooden plate—Maeve hefted a small stool, a determined look on her face.

She glanced to see what Myrtle had found, then frowned.

"Where's Myrtle?" she glanced around the room. No, she wasn't mistaken. Myrtle was not amongst them. Something dark and ugly unfurled inside her, a toxic anxiety that was nearly paralysing.

Sweet, young Myrtle. "Where is she?" she rasped.

Maeve frowned. "Last I saw, she was heading for the kitchen."

Cook shook her head. "I dinna see her."

Brenda strode toward the door. "Maeve, you're in charge. Don't let anyone past this door unless you know him directly."

Gwennie made a small whimper, and tried to grab on to her skirts. Brenda leaned over and held her by her shoulders.

"I have to find Myrtle, Gwennie," she said quietly, understanding the child's distress. "You are safe here. Maeve will look after you, and I'm going down the stairs—nobody will get past me unless I allow it. You are safe."

She glanced at Maeve, and the maid nodded, hefting the stool.

"Lock the door behind me," she said sharply as she strode from the room. She paused in the hall until she heard the lock engage, and even smiled briefly when she heard Maeve giving instructions for the women to move a chest in front of the door. She walked across the landing to the sound of moving furniture in the chamber she'd just left.

She withdrew her short sword, holding it in front of her with both hands as she crept along down the stairs. Her heart pounding, she carefully peered around each bend before she padded down the next flight. She eventually reached the ground floor, and stared along the length of the great hall. There were a great many tables and bench seats about, providing plenty of hiding spots for a psychopathic killer. There were also several alcoves along the sides of the hall, some with doors leading to other parts of the castle.

The place was a damn maze.

She stepped carefully into the hall, opting to walk down the centre aisle. It gave little cover, but it afforded her the best view of those alcoves. Her boots crunched on the reeds on the floor, and she gritted her teeth, trying to tread lightly.

She leaned down to check under the tables and chairs, and could see nobody huddling in that space. Swinging her sword in one direction, then the other, she carefully made her way down the aisle, warily eyeing the darker spaces beyond.

She was about half way down the hall when she heard it. A sniffle. She froze, waiting, listening.

There it was again, a sniffle, and perhaps harsh breathing.

The doors to the great hall swung open, and Duncan bounded in and down the steps, skidding to stop when he saw her standing in the middle, her finger to her lips.

He held up a hand and his men halted behind him. She pointed to one of the alcoves on her right, Duncan's left, and started to walk in that direction.

Duncan also started to walk toward her, reaching behind to draw his broadsword from the sheath strapped to his back, and a shorter blade from his belt.

Together they advanced toward the shadowy niche. As soon as Brenda could see into the entire area, she halted, dismayed.

Myrtle stared at her, eyes wide, tears streaming down her cheeks, as Maxwell's grubby hand covered her mouth, another holding a knife to her throat.

"Well, well, Enforcer," Maxwell rasped. "You are full of surprises. Here I thought you'd perished in that battle we encountered on our arrival in this time, when you've actually been playing lady of the manor."

"Let her go." Duncan's voice was a low, deep rumble, full of lethal intent.

Maxwell rubbed his cheek against Myrtle's face, and the young girl whimpered. Brenda wanted to run to her and yank her out of the psychopath's clutches—and she'd only known the girl for a few days. She couldn't imagine the torment Duncan must be going through.

She took a step to the side, slowly fanning out so that it was difficult for Maxwell to keep them both in his direct line of sight. Duncan started to do the same.

"That's enough, Enforcer," the man shouted.

"Let the girl go, Maxwell," she said to him quietly, calmly.

"Drop your weapons, all of you," Maxwell shouted, "or I'll kill her. Ask your lady, here. She'll tell you I mean business."

Brenda's jaw clenched. Damn it. He was too far away. If they tried to rush him, he could slit Myrtle's throat before they reached him. She could see the whites of his eyes, he was feeling the frenzy again.

She nodded, darting a quick glance at Duncan.

"Let her go, and this man will let you plead his case."

She ignored Duncan's snort.

"Drop your sword, Enforcer," Maxwell shouted, and he pressed the blade harder against Myrtle's neck, drawing blood.

Duncan's sword dropped to the ground with a clang, and he waved for his kinsmen to do the same.

Brenda reluctantly followed suit, then raised her now-empty hands and stepped closer to the man.

"We've done as you asked, now let her go."

She couldn't quite see him out of the corner of her eye, but she felt the shift in the air currents around her. Duncan was also moving. She refused to ponder how she could be so aware of the man's whereabouts, his actions.

Maxwell tried to back up further, coming up against the stone wall.

"I urge you to let the lass go," Duncan said softly, and even Brenda shivered at the menace in his tone.

Maxwell's gaze darted between the two of them, and she could see the beginnings of a sinister smile. That's not good.

"Myrtle, do you remember that dance I taught you?" she asked calmly.

Myrtle's brow furrowed, and she nodded, once, in confusion.

"Remember it by the numbers?" she asked softly. "One, two, three, four." She nodded at the girl, trying to communicate her intention. "But don't forget the bow at the end."

Myrtle whimpered as Maxwell shifted, and Brenda felt sick at the sight of the thin trail of blood that dripped down Myrtle's neck from the small cut. She took a deep breath, hoping the young woman did her bidding, was brave enough to take the action Brenda so desperately hoped she would. She started to clap, ignoring the frown Duncan shot at her, keeping her stare connected with Myrtle's. She created a steady rhythm, then nodded.

"One." Her voice was strong and forceful. "Two. Three. Four!"

Just as they'd practiced, Myrtle executed the moves. Strike. Twist. Kick. Evade. Maxwell bellowed as Myrtle's fist punched him fiercely in the groin, then yowled when she gripped his wrist and twisted it as she spun out. Her soft-booted foot kicked his knee in at an unnatural angle, and she jerked away.

Brenda acted instantly, reaching behind her for the knife at her back. She brought her hand through and flung the knife. It was instantaneous and it was lethal. Maxwell's cry was cut short as he collapsed to the ground. Two blades protruded, Brenda's from his neck, and Duncan's from his heart. Brenda's eyes widened. Duncan had thrown the knife she'd given him—so quickly, and so true.

Duncan swept Myrtle into his arms and away from the dead man, soothing her as he turned her away from the scene. His gaze found Brenda's over his sister's head. He gave her a small nod, conveying gratitude as well as acknowledgement.

Gareth bounded over, placing his hand on Myrtle's shoulder, his face lined with worry and relief.

Brenda hung there for a moment, feeling awkward and gauche at the intimate moment.

She gestured casually over her shoulder. "I'll, uh, I'll head up to the women," she said to nobody in particular.

"Brenda, I am so grateful," Myrtle called over her shoulder, extending an arm out toward her. Duncan shifted and also raised his arm, his green gaze dark with a tender warmth that spread through her gawky little heart like a warm tide, washing some of the pain out of dark memories, and awakening something new.

Brenda stepped forward cautiously, but all it took was that one step, and she was swept up into the embrace as the rest of the men cheered.

Oh. Um. Hm. For a moment she wasn't quite sure what to do with her arms, but hesitantly raised them.

She was surrounded by warmth, by relief, and generous support—and for a moment that was ever so brief, she felt like she was home.

Chapter Ten

Brenda stared in awe at the party before her. Maxwell's body had been removed and Myrtle's near brush with death was apparently enough of an excuse to hold a feast. The great hall was full of Gordon clan members who were gathered to celebrate Myrtle's rescue, and to honour the passing of Davey with a respect and a joy and determination that was fascinating. Musicians played strange instruments, and Cook was delivering a banquet that threatened to collapse the tables that bore it.

She patted her tummy. Good grief, she was stuffed. She winked at little Gwennie who was stealing yet another mince pie from Duncan's plate. The little girl was still quiet and contained, but every now and then Brenda spied a cheeky little sprite when she relaxed.

"Show us your dance," Gareth yelled, and the cheer was quickly taken up by the rest of the men in the hall. Duncan reached for her hand and grasped it, smiling.

"Aye, please show us this dance of yours," he encouraged her.

She eyed him for a moment, considering her options, before finally nodding. "Okay. If all the ladies agree?" she called out, smiling mischievously at the gathering. The women clapped and squealed, and Brenda rose as the men started to clear the tables.

"But we'll each need a partner," she said, raising her voice, and the women laughed as they carefully selected their partners. She gestured to the musicians and clapped out a rhythm, and the makeshift band started to play a merry tune. She tugged on Duncan's hand.

"Will you do me the honour, kind sir?" she asked, curtseying deeply, and tripping on her skirt as she rose.

Duncan caught her and rolled his eyes before laughing. "Aye, it would be my pleasure."

He followed her down to the cleared space, shaking his long dark hair back as he took up the position she showed him.

"Okay, ladies, let me count you in," she called out, tapping her boot to the rhythm and sharing secretive smiles with the women. She had to focus on the music, and not on the warmth of Duncan's body so close to her own. "One, two, three, four."

And in perfect synchronisation, the Gordon women performed their martial moves on the Gordon warriors. There were plenty of surprised yells and bellows as the men hit the floor, followed by shrieks of laughter as the woman clapped.

Brenda chuckled at Duncan's shocked gaze from his position on the floor, before she squealed in surprise as he jerked her down on top of him.

"'Tis a feisty lass you are," he whispered, smiling against her lips, and he kissed her briefly. "And 'tis proud I am to call you wife."

Brenda felt a warmth bloom in her chest that was part attraction, and yet so much more. She gazed down at the strong, dark warrior beneath her, ignoring the laughter and cheers of the crowd around her. This man, who fought with so much dedication and determination for his family, whose protection and loyalty seemed forged from steel, and whose sense of honour and duty mirrored her own, claimed her as his. And it thrilled her.

"As I am proud to call you husband."

His smile faltered, his gaze shifted, and he sighed. "I must show you something," he murmured, as he set her aside and rose, then turned to offer her his hand.

She frowned. He'd gone so serious all of a sudden. She accepted his grasp, allowing him to pull her gently to her feet.

He led her from the hall, waving at the rest of the kinfolk as they continued to dance merrily into the night. He drew her down the passage that led to the storerooms, hefting a torch from its brace as he did so.

He raised the torch a little, using it to light the corridor and stairs. He had to walk stooped over, his frame almost too large to fit in the confines of the paths below the castle, all the way to the storeroom where he'd hidden her weapons.

She frowned. Okay, so this wasn't some little ploy to get her away from the crowd so they could consummate their marriage—and she was surprised at the brief flare of disappointment at the thought. Oh, hell, was he going to imprison her, after all?

DUNCAN SET THE FLAMING torch in the wall brace, then crossed to a small box and hesitated, his hand resting on the lid. Hell. This was so difficult. He turned to her, and she gazed at him warily, a line marring her brow, the smiles and warmth of just a few moments ago were gone. With good reason, alas.

"I've lied to you, lass, and I'm sorry." There. 'Twas like chewing nails. He dinna like the taste those words left in his mouth, or what he had to do.

Her frown deepened, her confusion clear. "Is this handfasting business just a joke?" she asked.

He gaped at her, then frowned. "No! 'Tis no jest." Did she wish that? Oh, God, was he going to lose her?

"What is it?" she whispered.

"I want you to know, I thought it was for the best," he said roughly, his voice almost a whisper. "When that bastard had Myrtle, my heart was so sore," he told her, his hand rising to rub at his chest, and he grimaced at the remembered pain. "She's my only family and for a moment I came close to losing her." It had been then that he'd realised. He'd stolen Brenda from her family.

After everything he'd endured, with all the taunts and rumours, the broken betrothals and the almost desperate desire to find a mate, he finally had what he wanted most—but he couldn't keep her.

Brenda averted her gaze. "I'm sorry," she whispered to him.

"Nay, you have no need for regret," he said, surprised. "It made me realise what you must feel, being trapped here," he told her quietly. "I dinna like the feel of it, and I doona want you to feel that." He finally had a bride, but he'd tricked her, taken advantage of her ignorance ... he wanted her, wanted her desperately, but he wanted her to want him, otherwise he wanted nothing.

He sighed. "You are so different, Brenda. Your ways—" he smiled, "you canna wear our clothes without issue." He gestured to the skirts, still caught up in the belt, exposing her legs from the knees down.

Brenda's cheeks flushed. "I keep tripping," she responded. "But I can try." She tugged at the fabric caught by her belt, but he reached over to stop her. Damn, he'd hurt her feelings, mayhap embarrassed her. That was no' his intent.

"Nay, lass. I happen to like you even more for it." He stepped closer and dipped his head, his frank gaze meeting hers. "Why were you hunting this Maxwell?" He needed to hear her say it again. He had his suspicions, and if he could, he would ignore them, but it wasna just him that would be affected.

She clasped her hands together in front of her. "It's my duty," she said quietly, and he frowned. She'd used those words afore, in his chamber. "This is what I do."

He ducked his head. And there it was. No woman of his experience did what Brenda did. Nor did they speak as she did, fight like she did, nor protect like she did. He'd finally found a woman he would readily lay down his life for, who shared the same ideals, who could understand him as no other ... and he'd captured her through lies. He couldna do it. Wouldna do it.

He cleared his throat, his fingers rubbing the lid of the box. "I know you're no' from around here." He met her blue gaze, dark with confusion, with anxiety. "I know family is important and I doona want to keep you from yours. I love you, Brenda Gordon, and I want you to stay, but only if you wish it."

He lifted the lid and showed her what was inside. Her gasp was clearly audible in the small storeroom as she gazed down. The strange little box Maxwell had tried to use lay nestled inside. He'd lied to her when he'd told her it had fallen down a ravine. It had been a desperate attempt to keep her with him, to hold her close, to start a life—but not like this. He glanced down at the funny little thing. It was similar to Brenda's one that Gareth had destroyed, and he knew it was her key to go home.

He started to turn away, sadness weighing heavily on his shoulders, but Brenda's hand stopped him. He turned back to her, dismayed at the tears in her eyes.

"You would let me leave—because you love me?" she asked, tilting her head, a confused frown marring her brow.

He nodded, even though his heart was breaking. "Aye."

She shook her head. "I don't understand your logic, warrior, but I think I appreciate it."

She looked at the box, her expression clearly torn. Duncan clenched his jaw. She dinna say she loved him.

He started to back away. He had to leave. He dinna want to wait for her to perform whatever spell she cast to return from whence she came, to disappear from his life. He remembered the worry, the concern he'd felt when Colleen's absence was first noticed, then the regret when they'd found her body, and the realisation she'd taken her life to avoid sharing his.

Those emotions, though, paled into insignificance in the face of the depth of his feelings today—for Brenda, at the prospect of losing her.

"Wait," she said, and he turned. She was smiling.

He frowned. His heart was nigh in two and she was smiling?

"I came here to catch a man, and I thought I had no way to return to my time. You tricked me into marrying you." She folded her arms and walked toward him. "Then you left me here."

He dipped his head. It sounded harsh when she said it like that.

She paused in front of him, her gaze considering, before she tilted her head. "And I've never felt so at home in all my life," she told him softly, unfolding her arms so that she could clasp his face between her hands. "When I thought Gwennie might be in danger, then saw Maxwell had Myrtle, I was so worried." She swallowed. "Let me be clear—this is the kind of thing I do, and I do it well, but that was the first time I lost my objectivity," she whispered, her eyes wide. "I was so scared for Myrtle, and for you."

His eyebrows rose. "For me?"

"Yes. I know how important your family is to you." She lowered her hands, but he caught them, holding them. He had no idea what the lass was trying to say, but he wanted to hold on to her for as long as possible.

"I want—" She hesitated, then sucked in a breath. "I want to be that important to someone," she whispered in a rush, her gaze searching his. "I want what you have here. I want to be part—"

He cut off her words with a kiss. He'd heard enough, and finally figured out what the lass was trying to say. She wanted him.

"I love you, Brenda," he whispered between kisses.

"I love you, too, Duncan," she whispered right back. He pulled her tight against him, then grimaced at the sharp prick of pain in his thigh. He set back a little.

"What is that?"

She was already fumbling with the cord at her thighs. "Sorry, that's my blade." There was a clatter on the stone floor as she dropped it.

He smiled and waggled his eyebrows. "Och, I've got a blade for you," he whispered, and pressed his lips against hers as her arms slid around his waist, his pulse hammering—until she whimpered, jerking back.

"What's that?" she asked, gesturing to his side.

He winced. "Sorry, love, that's my dirk," he whispered, pulling the blade from the sheath at his waist, letting it join hers on the floor.

He pulled her to him, kissing her as he bore her back against a pile of burlap bags, desire tightening his muscles, each disarming the other as they encountered more uncomfortable moments with their personal arsenals. Her breasts pressed against his chest, and he moaned as his groin settled against the warmth of her core, the rough burlap creating a friction against his legs.

He hesitated, and she groaned in frustration. "Now, what?" she growled, her face flushed with the same arousal that was fast consuming him.

"You're my bride, lass. We should be doing this in a bed, with soft—" His words were cut off as she yanked on his hair and pulled him down for her kiss.

"Screw the bed," she muttered as she pressed kisses against his jaw and neck.

"Och, we can screw the bed, and any other room you wish," he muttered back as he dragged at the laces of her bodice.

She tugged on his shirt, and he paused to allow her to pull the garment over his head. "I notice there are a lot of rooms in this castle," she said, and he nodded as he pulled the bodice down over her breasts, revealing pretty pink nipples that puckered under his gaze.

"Aye, and we can screw in every one," he said, dipping his head to capture a rosy peak in his mouth.

She quivered against him, her head rolling back as she moaned her pleasure. After all their kisses, all their shared embraces, he was ready to explode. He couldn't believe how fast and how thoroughly this woman managed to arouse him.

He pulled at her skirts, finally realising a benefit to the unique manner in which she wore her garb. Brenda's movements were just as hurried as she tugged at his kilt, and he rolled the nipple in his mouth as he caressed her beneath her skirts.

"I can't wait any longer," she panted, when she finally grasped him. He lifted his head at the intense bliss her touch gave him, and saw her eyes widen. He grinned as he moved a little, and she guided him to her entrance, their gazes caught as he slid inside her with silken ease.

He shuddered, closing his eyes at the bliss that enveloped him. "It's like coming home," he whispered, sheathing himself to the hilt.

She smiled. "Exactly," she whispered. "Welcome home."

They made love, ignoring the revelry above stairs, the cold stone chamber surrounding them—they generated enough heat between them as they made this time their own.

The End.

About the Author

Once a dangerous goods handler, betting agent and administration manager, Shannon Curtis is now an award-winning author as well as a creative writing teacher at the Sydney Community College, and is published in contemporary romance, paranormal and suspense fiction. Her hobbies have ranged from lapidary, to knitting and embroidery (although crochet still defeats her), with a long-term interest in various forms of martial arts. When not reading or writing, Shannon spends her time with her supportive husband and three children, their dog, and a cat with way too much attitude. And watching way too much TV, movies and Netflix. Preferably with wine and chocolate on hand.

    1   2   3   4

SIGN UP FOR SHANNON'S newsletter[5].

    Email: contactme@shannoncurtis.com

    Website: www.shannoncurtis.com[6]

    Facebook: https://www.facebook.com/Shannon.Curtis.Writers.Ink/

    Twitter: @2BShannonCurtis[7]

    Instagram: ShannonCurtisWrites[8]

1. http://www.shannoncurtis.com/

2. https://www.facebook.com/Shannon.Curtis.Writers.Ink/

3. https://twitter.com/2BShannonCurtis

4. https://www.instagram.com/shannoncurtiswrites/?hl=en

5. http://eepurl.com/eaYa9

6.   http://www.shannoncurtis.com

7.   https://twitter.com/2BShannonCurtis

Book List
Contemporary Romance
The Bold and The Beautiful Series:
Collision Course[9]
Stormswept[10]
Sunset Love[11]
Romantic Suspense
McCormack Security Agency Series:
Vipers Kiss[12]
Guarding Jess[13]
For Her Eyes Only[14]
Knight Family Novels Series:
Runaway Lies[15]

---

9. https://www.amazon.com/Collision-Course-Beautiful-Shannon-Curtis-ebook/dp/B00H8KB5PE/ref=sr_1_fkmrnull_1?keywords=collision+course+shannon+curtis&qid=1552004285&s=gateway&sr=8-1-fkmrnull

10. https://www.amazon.com/Stormswept-Bold-Beautiful-Shannon-Curtis-ebook/dp/B00J78QBI6/ref=pd_sim_351_2/140-2308682-5744152?_encoding=UTF8&pd_rd_i=B00J78QBI6&pd_rd_r=a70cef10-4137-11e9-acad-c779d924d9c8&pd_rd_w=bEAmg&pd_rd_wg=NUHEj&pf_rd_p=90485860-83e9-4fd9-b838-b28a9b7fda30&pf_rd_r=QWE6FAQM70FYZYYPHTHD&psc=1&refRID=QWE6FAQM70FYZYYPHTHD

11. https://www.amazon.com/Sunset-Love-Beautiful-Shannon-Curtis-ebook/dp/B00OSNKFY6/ref=sr_1_1?keywords=sunset+love+shannon+curtis&qid=1552004402&s=digital-text&sr=1-1-catcorr

12. https://www.amazon.com/Vipers-Kiss-McCormack-Security-Agency-ebook/dp/B00DJLSE-CI/ref=sr_1_20?keywords=shannon+curtis&qid=1552004531&s=digital-text&sr=1-20

13. https://www.amazon.com/Guarding-Jess-McCormack-Security-Agency-ebook/dp/B00DJLSEQ4/ref=sr_1_13?keywords=shannon+curtis&qid=1552004564&s=digital-text&sr=1-13

14. https://www.amazon.com/Eyes-Only-McCormack-Security-Agency-ebook/dp/B00EFPNV48/ref=sr_1_9?keywords=shannon+curtis&qid=1552004564&s=digital-text&sr=1-9

Heart Breaker[16]
Stand Alone Novels
Hope Echoes[17]
Once Upon a Crime Novellas
Enamoured[18]
Enraptured[19]
Stand Alone Novellas
Mistletoe Maverick[20]
Saving Santa[21]
Warrior in Time
The Girl Who Saw Too Much[22]
Paranormal Romance
Tribal Law[23]

---

15. https://www.amazon.com/Runaway-Lies-Shannon-Curtis-ebook/dp/B00R5GSMY8/
ref=sr_1_10?keywords=shannon+curtis&qid=1552004564&s=digital-text&sr=1-10

16. https://www.amazon.com/Heart-Breaker-Shannon-Curtis-ebook/dp/B01NALOYVH/
ref=sr_1_3?keywords=shannon+curtis&qid=1552004564&s=digital-text&sr=1-3

17. https://www.amazon.com/Hope-Echoes-Echo-Springs-Book-ebook/dp/B07CJM8Z1G/
ref=sr_1_4?keywords=shannon+curtis&qid=1552005036&s=digital-text&sr=1-4

18. https://www.amazon.com/Enamoured-Once-Upon-Crime-Book-ebook/dp/B00BTTJ86I/
ref=sr_1_18?keywords=shannon+curtis&qid=1552005008&s=digital-text&sr=1-18

19. https://www.amazon.com/Enraptured-Once-Upon-Crime-Book-ebook/dp/B00LGDXI04/
ref=sr_1_7?keywords=shannon+curtis&qid=1552005036&s=digital-text&sr=1-7

20. https://www.amazon.com/Mistletoe-Maverick-Shannon-Curtis-ebook/dp/B019BG8VWM/
ref=sr_1_15?keywords=shannon+curtis&qid=1552004564&s=digital-text&sr=1-15

21. https://www.amazon.com/Saving-Santa-Christmas-Romantic-Suspense-ebook/dp/
B07H2JFHFJ/ref=sr_1_11?keywords=shannon+curtis&qid=1552004564&s=digital-text&sr=1-11

22. https://www.amazon.com/Girl-Who-Saw-Too-Much-ebook/dp/B07N972KTF/
ref=sr_1_2?keywords=shannon+curtis&qid=1552004564&s=digital-text&sr=1-2

23. https://www.amazon.com/Tribal-Law-Miscreants-Magick-Book-ebook/dp/B00SDRM0SW/
ref=sr_1_14?keywords=shannon+curtis&qid=1552005036&s=digital-text&sr=1-14

Lycan Unleashed[24]
Warrior Untamed[25]
Vampire Undone[26]
Wolf Undaunted[27]
Witch Hunter[28]
Once Upon a Crime Novellas
Enamoured[29]
Enraptured[30]
Stand Alone Novellas
Warrior of the Realm[31]

24. https://www.amazon.com/Lycan-Unleashed-Shannon-Curtis-ebook/dp/B01JOCBFDU/
ref=sr_1_24?keywords=shannon+curtis&qid=1552005679&s=digital-text&sr=1-24

25. https://www.amazon.com/Warrior-Untamed-Shannon-Curtis-ebook/dp/B01MFGQ1E3/
ref=sr_1_19?keywords=shannon+curtis&qid=1552005679&s=digital-text&sr=1-19

26. https://www.amazon.com/Vampire-Undone-Shannon-Curtis-ebook/dp/B075WTKLK9/
ref=sr_1_22?keywords=shannon+curtis&qid=1552005679&s=digital-text&sr=1-22

27. https://www.amazon.com/Wolf-Undaunted-Shannon-Curtis-ebook/dp/B079ZYQ3PD/
ref=sr_1_17?keywords=shannon+curtis&qid=1552005679&s=digital-text&sr=1-17

28. https://www.amazon.com/Witch-Hunter-Shannon-Curtis-ebook/dp/B07C76DSC4/
ref=sr_1_23?keywords=shannon+curtis&qid=1552005679&s=digital-text&sr=1-23

29. https://www.amazon.com/Enamoured-Once-Upon-Crime-Book-ebook/dp/B00BTTJ86I/
ref=sr_1_18?keywords=shannon+curtis&qid=1552005008&s=digital-text&sr=1-18

30. https://www.amazon.com/Enraptured-Once-Upon-Crime-Book-ebook/dp/B00LGDXI04/
ref=sr_1_7?keywords=shannon+curtis&qid=1552005036&s=digital-text&sr=1-7

31. https://www.harlequin.com/shop/articles/339_warrior-of-the-realm.html

Looking for another read?
Check out this excerpt from The Girl Who Saw Too Much, Available now![32]

The Girl Who Saw Too Much

By Shannon Curtis

"Will you give me that," Indie said, trying not to snap as she snatched her laser pointer from Max, her fourteen-year-old nephew. "It's not a toy."

"Aw, come on, Aunt Indie. It's fun. It's kind of like a gun sight."

"But it's not, and yes, seeing people freak and dive is amusing, but when the cops start knocking on my door and I send them your way, you won't think it's so funny. Besides, do you know how much damage that thing can do to an eye?"

"Sorry, Aunt Indie," her nephew mumbled, but his grin showed how unrepentant he was.

Indie rolled her eyes as she maneuvered her wheelchair through the sliding balcony door and into her small one-bedroom apartment. That's getting smaller by the minute. She watched her sister fuss over the work files scattered across the couch. Her other nephew, Mark, tossed his basketball in the air and caught it just before it hit her Willow Tree figurine collection.

Don't say anything, damn it. They're here for a visit. She should appreciate the intrusion ... er, company.

"Hey, Aunt Indie, do you have any neighbors yet?" Mark asked.

"Not yet, but I heard someone moved into the corner apartment on level eight."

Hers was a new building, and so far only about ten percent of the apartments had been sold. It was kind of eerie, knowing she was the only person for two floors.

"Just leave it, Paris, the couch is fine. Everything is fine." There, she'd managed to keep the irritation out of her voice as her sister organized the files into neat stacks that would take her at least half an hour to sort out later. Remember, she's only trying to help.

Really.

Her sister frowned. "Are you sure? Do you want me to do some laundry? Clean your bathroom?"

Indie smiled. "Seriously? I'm fine. I can do my own laundry, and the bathroom is fine. Everything is fine." If she kept saying it, she might start to believe it. After four weeks of being stuck in a wheelchair, stuck in an apartment in a brand-new, still-to-be-occupied apartment block, she was fluctuating between wanting to get out and socialize, and wanting to be left the hell alone.

She placed the laser pointer on the coffee table. She practiced her workshop presentations on her living room wall with her digital projector. After this recuperative stint, the projector wouldn't be needed in the workshops as she'd be able to recite all the details by rote. At least she'd remembered to pack away that expensive piece of equipment before her nephews had arrived.

Paris collapsed on the couch. "No, everything is not fine, and you know it." She gestured to the wheelchair. "How long have you got left in that thing?"

Too bloody long. "Two more weeks. Then I get to go on to crutches, hopefully."

"I'm so sorry," Paris whispered, for what seemed like the sixty-seven millionth time over the last four weeks.

Indie waved her hand. "It's fine, Paris. It was an accident."

Yeah. An accident where she'd wound up with two broken legs, thank you very much. Not one, two! She'd taken her nephews to the local skate park and they'd accidentally knocked her off the top of a ramp with their tomfoolery. She still hadn't lived it down at work. She, Indiana Phelps, organized, conservative training officer, had broken both her legs on a skateboard ramp. She'd laugh herself, if it wasn't so painful. And humiliating. She was finally able to dismiss her private nurse and look after her own needs. Two more weeks in the wheelchair and then she'd be free. Free!

She checked her watch. "While I love your company, Sis, and the two ferals," she jerked her head to the boys now wrestling just inside the balcony doorway, "isn't Mark due at his soccer presentation?"

"Boys, stop it! If you break anything, you're paying for it!" Paris shot to her feet. She, too, glanced at her watch. "Yeah, I guess. I just don't want to leave you alone."

A vase wobbled on the coffee table as one of the boys nudged it while attempting to get his brother in a headlock. Oh, please, leave me alone. Indie smiled.

"I'm fine. Really." Four weeks of imposed rest and recuperation had made her appreciate the quiet times.

Mark stumbled against her bookshelf and a couple of books fell down. She wasn't normally a recluse but the concept was growing more attractive by the minute.

"Boys! I swear I can't take you anywhere." Paris pulled her teenage sons apart and ushered them to the door. She paused at the end of the corridor and pointed to the telescope on its stand. "How is Mr. Hunka-licious going?"

The boys made kissing noises until their mother glared them into silence.

Indie's cheeks reddened. She now regretted showing her sister her neighboring eye candy. "Fine."

Paris smiled knowingly. "Uh-huh. Are you going to ask him out?"

Indie shook her head. "Good-bye, Paris."

"You're right. I think he would be a splendid kisser."

Indie clapped her hand over her eyes. "I shouldn't have told you that."

"Hey, I'm just wondering what else you haven't told me about your fantasies of Mr. Hunkalicious."

"Are you still here?"

Paris chuckled as she picked up her handbag and keys from the dining table and herded her sons. "I never realized you were such a voyeur."

"You started it!" Indie shot back as her sister left.

If possible, Indie's cheeks grew hotter. She wasn't a voyeur. Not really. Her sister had given her the telescope as a guilty gift to help her through her confinement. She looked at the stars, darn it all. She was here by herself – what else was a woman with a healthy sense of curiosity to do? So what if the lens occasionally dipped to spy on the few neighbors in the building. There was some pretty weird crap going on in this estate.

There was the old lady on the third level whom Indie had affectionately named Miss Kitty, due to her six cats – and her habit of sharing her dinner with her pets. Literally. Then there was Vacuum Dude, the guy who liked to vacuum in the nude every Friday night on level six. Indie shuddered delicately at the thought. One day he was going to hurt himself. But she'd hit pay dirt with Mr. Hunkalicious on level fourteen, two levels below her. Tall and hunky, he came home in a corporate suit and then changed into shorts and t-shirt. Or on a good day, just shorts. With messy dark hair, scruffy and relaxed, he was gorgeous. Indie preferred the scruffy look. Much sexier. Especially on a good day. It had been a really good day, two days ago. He'd come out of his bathroom wearing nothing but a towel and went straight over to his balcony door to look out. She'd nearly fallen out of her chair when he'd tugged the towel from his waist to dry his hair.

But she was not a voyeur.

Turning her wheelchair around, she made her clumsy way to the kitchen, bumping into furniture her nephews had moved. Did they do it on purpose? They must. Moving her cumbersome chair this way and that, she maneuvered around the small space in an effort to prepare dinner. She pulled a carton of eggs out of the fridge then had to reverse in order to close the fridge door. She twisted to the side to grab the handle, and the carton slid off her lap to the floor with a distinct splat.

She eyed the yellow mess on the tiles sourly.

I am so looking forward to crutches.

SEVERAL HOURS LATER she closed her laptop. Ugh. At this rate, she'd have the next twelve months' presentations done, and wouldn't actually have anything left to do when she returned to work. She glanced at her watch.

"Oh!" She set her laptop aside with a clunk, and wheeled her chair over to the window. She'd almost forgotten. There was a lunar eclipse tonight. Ever since Paris had given her the telescope, she'd researched as many constellations and celestial events as possible.

"Good old Google," she murmured as she got into position and pulled the lens to her eye. So far, all the constellations just looked like a bunch of stars. How anyone could make out a saucepan from a collection of twinkling lights was beyond her, but she should be able to recognize an eclipse, right?

She angled the lens upwards. Clouds. Stars. Where's the moon? She pulled back, looked up, and oriented herself. Of course, that massive glowing orb over there. She lined up the telescope and looked again. Wow. It was – um, only just beginning, apparently. There was a dark smudge on the lower right quadrant. She sat back. So, what, another half hour or so before the earth's shadow centered on the moon and created an eerie red ring?

She frowned. "Or is it the sun's shadow?" She couldn't remember. Well, if she had some time, what to do? She leaned in and re-focused the telescope on the building face opposite. The apartment block was built in an L-shape, with two elevators in the middle of each block, and a maintenance-only lift in the corner.

"Oh, Miss Kitty, is that ice cream?" Indie watched as the old woman let one of her cats lick the spoon before putting it back in the container and pulling out some more. "Ick."

She moved the lens again and sought out Vacuum Dude. It was Saturday night, not Friday, so thankfully no vacuuming. She counted down to level six. Oh, look, he's got some mates over playing poker. Oh, look, they're lighting their farts. She shook her head in exasperation and swiveled the lens to two levels below her own.

Whoa.

Two short, stocky guys wearing black balaclavas held Mr. Hunkalicious, while another taller, leaner masked man punched him in the gut.

Indie blinked. What? She looked again. Yes, she'd seen right. Mr. Hunkalicious was being attacked. Her jaw dropped and she sat up straight.

Whoa.

She had to call for help. She looked frantically for her phone. There! On the floor, by the bookcase. She rolled her chair over to it, leaned down and picked it up. She tried to dial but nothing came up on the screen. She shook the phone. Dead. It was dead, damn it! Her nephews must have pressed it on during their wrestle. Crap. Her mobile phone was at work. Her supervisor had insisted that as it was a work phone, it should stay at work while she recuperated. Jerk.

She pushed her chair over to the telescope again, fumbling frantically to peer through the lens. There he was, struggling against three men.

By the time she wheeled herself into the lift and got down to the lobby payphone, he could be dead. Her gaze fell upon the laser pointer she'd placed on the coffee table earlier. Maybe … ?

Pushing her wheels as hard and as fast as she could, she rolled over to the coffee table and snatched the pointer up. Reversing, she swore at her clumsiness. A growl of frustration escaped as she bumped into the doorframe, and then hauled to a stop on her balcony. Using the sight on her telescope, she lined up her laser pointer and turned it on.

Like a stream of righteous red anger, the laser beam pierced the night. She peered through the lens of the telescope, angling the pointer until a red dot appeared on Mr. Hunkalicious's white shirt.

One of the men holding Mr. Hunkalicious froze then spoke rapidly to the other guy who was clenching his fist, ready to strike again. She slowly moved the beam so that the red dot trailed from the white shirt to the black vest of the man holding him.

The man with the fist flinched, while the shorter man with the red dot on his chest dived backward. Mr. Hunkalicious swung into action, punching the man in the face then using his startled opponent as a battering ram on the man who had been beating him. Both dark figures fell to the floor and Mr. Hunkalicious bolted from the apartment.

Indie trained the laser beam on his assailants, watching with satisfaction as they dived behind furniture to dodge an imaginary bullet that would never be fired. One of the men finally made it out of the apartment in pursuit of Mr. Hunkalicious and Indie hoped she'd given him enough of a head start to escape.

Finally, one of the intruders peered over the back of the couch. She trained the laser beam to the top of his head, and waited for him to drop down again. Only, he didn't. Indie frowned. They both waited. Finally, he slowly rose from behind the couch, gesturing to the other guy hiding behind the curtain. The curtain twitched and the man emerged from his cover. They both looked up toward Indie.

Crap.

Belatedly, Indie realized she should have turned her living room light off. Her apartment would be shining like a beacon in the surrounding darkness of the unoccupied units.

Heart pounding, she watched through the lens as they pointed at her section of the building. They were calculating which floor she was on.

Double crap.

The taller man made a pretend gun out of his thumb and forefinger and pointed it at Indie and made a shooting motion with his hand. Her blood chilled in her veins. Both men turned and ran out of the apartment.

They were coming for her.

Indie whipped her gaze from the telescope and frantically wheeled herself off the balcony and through her living room. She grabbed her handbag from the kitchen counter as she barreled down the hall to her front door.

"Oh, crap," she wailed as she got to her door. She tried to open it but the footrest for the wheelchair was in the way. She had to roll back, lean forward and try again. She backed the wheelchair up as she pulled the door open.

A figure loomed in her doorway and she screamed.

Grab your copy of The Girl Who Saw Too Much today![33]

---

33. https://www.amazon.com/Girl-Who-Saw-Too-Much-ebook/dp/B07N972KTF/

ref=sr_1_2?keywords=shannon+curtis&qid=1552006404&s=digital-text&sr=1-2

Don't miss out!

Visit the website below and you can sign up to receive emails whenever Shannon Curtis publishes a new book. There's no charge and no obligation.

https://books2read.com/r/B-A-OJKC-QRSU

BOOKS 2 READ

Connecting independent readers to independent writers.